HARVEY
the
BEER CAN KING

HARVEY
the
BEER CAN KING

by Jamie Gilson

Illustrated by John Wallner

Lothrop, Lee & Shepard Company

A Division of William Morrow & Co., Inc. • New York

First Edition
1 2 3 4 5 6 7 8 9 10

Library of Congress Cataloging in Publication Data

Gilson, Jamie.
    Harvey, the beer can king.
    SUMMARY: A twelve-year-old boy hopes his beer can collection
will win him the title of sixth-grade Superkid.
    [1. Collectors and collecting—Fiction]
I. Wallner, John C. II. Title.
PZ7.G4385Har   [Fic]   78-1807
ISBN 0-688-41845-7
ISBN 0-688-51845-1 lib. bdg.

To Tom, Matthew and Anne—Superkids.

Contents

1 · Superkids

I used to like Quint Calkins, even though I hardly knew him. If you'd asked me which kid he was, I'd have told you he was the guy with the long black bangs, the kid who could curl his lip way up on one side like he smelled skunk. (I'm not saying that's bad. It's terrific. I'd do it myself if I could.) I knew he gave good birthday presents—stuff like monster models and plastic ice cubes with flies in them. He liked magic. He was better than anybody else at running the hundred. And that's about all I knew.

So when he told me one day in gym that he knew all about beer cans, I told him I had the best collection in town. Why be modest, right? And when he said his dad had just brought him two Pike's Peak Ales from Colorado, I asked him if he wanted to trade. "Sure," he said. "Why not?"

After school I bagged a few fairly choice cans and skateboarded down the hill to the park. Quint was already there. He was sitting on top of the high slide, holding a big brown grocery bag in his lap. And he was curling his lip at the line of little kids waiting behind him. Quint's a big guy, a lot taller than me, and those kindergarten kids couldn't budge him.

"Go away, insects. I *live* up here," Quint said,

leaning back on the line of them. "I'm king of this mountain." The kids on the slide stomped on the steps and shouted. This really little girl threw her big yellow beach ball at him. It almost hit his shoes. Quint sneered at her and started roaring down.

"Godzilla!" somebody on the slide steps shrieked. Quint turned on the group of them, whipping the sack around over his head. I could hear metal crashing inside.

"Hey, Quint," I yelled at him. "You got your cans in there?" I thought maybe I could stop a riot. Besides, I didn't want to trade for any beat-up cans.

He looked over, surprised to see me. "Naw," he said, really sarcastic. "I got a baby rattle, can't you see?" He shook his sack at the kid who'd thrown the ball. She kicked at it and missed. "I scare infants with it." He flung it up, grabbed it just before it hit the ground, and then tossed it over to me.

We sat on a grassy patch away from the slides and emptied our cans out among the dandelions. If Quint had a great collection he sure hadn't brought any of it with him. They were just cans like you'd find in park bushes after any old warm Saturday night. Only one was halfway decent. But I figured I might as well give the guy a chance.

"Quint," I told him. "This is your lucky day. You give me that Pike's Peak Ale and I'll trade you a Schlitz Malt, a Lone Star, and a seven-ounce Rolling Rock." I was *giving* them away. "OK?"

He flipped the hair out of his eyes and looked them over. When he found a scratch on the Rolling Rock, he looked up at me so I could see his lip arch in disgust. "Oh, why not?" he said finally.

"I'll tell you why I'm giving you three for one." I didn't want him to think I was a pushover. "They're doubles, that's why. And I've got to start cutting my collection." One of the kids from the slide ran by and stuck out her tongue. We ignored her.

"Cutting it?" he asked. "Why would you want to do that?"

I didn't *want* to, that's for sure. "Oh, my mom gave me the old Beer Can Lecture again this morning. The same old stuff about how she's put up with it long enough now and, Harvey Trumble, you get those smelly cans off the floor and into the trash. 'I mean it this time,' she said."

Quint dug a flat rusty Schlitz out of the bushes and arced it toward the trash barrel. It hit the edge and bounced in. Lucky. "Two points, star. Did she mean it?" he asked, as if he didn't care worth a rusty can whether she did or not.

"Probably not." She was always after me about them. But she's a pussycat. I lay back in the grass, resting the old head on the skateboard, rolling it back and forth to massage my brain muscles. "I'll tell her at supper that I've taken her advice and started trading down. That'll do it."

"Look, you really want to get rid of them?" Quint

asked, a little too quickly. "I'll take them off your hands for nothing."

You bet he would. He'd take them off my hands, put them in paper bags, and whip them around at little kids. "No thanks," I told him. "I'm just bluffing her. I won't trade down far."

I really like those cans. I think it's great how they come from Japan and New Jersey and all those little towns in Wisconsin and how they stack up in silver

towers in my room. I stretched out in the grass feeling good. "I like having more of them than anybody else. I wouldn't give them up for anything."

A bicycle skidded right in front of us and Suzanna Brooks, this whiz kid on wheels with the paper route, slid to a stop on the grass. Suzanna can ride a unicycle as easy as most kids can walk, but she needed a bicycle basket for the paper route. She took a newspaper out of her basket and asked, "You guys running?"

"Nope, jogging," Quint said.

"Hang-gliding," I told her.

"Free-falling?" Quint asked, collapsing spread eagle on the ground.

Suzanna looked annoyed. "I mean, how about running in the *Examiner*'s new contest? It tells all about it in today's paper."

Quint lay there on the ground with his eyes closed, fake laughing. "Come on, Suze, tell us the truth. How much extra do they pay you to push those stupid contests?"

"Forget it," I told her. "Thanks, but no thanks." The *Examiner* is our town's newspaper. It's *always* having contests about something. In the fall it's an Apple Pie Recipe Contest. Last winter they had a Snow Person Building Contest. Sometimes they just put photographs in the paper to see who can tell what the picture is of—stuff like very close close-ups of paper clips or an ant's eye. Once my brother won their Piano Playing Contest, though, and they gave him this really neat Scott Joplin record.

My dad says the *Examiner* has all these contests because the rest of the news they print is so dull. I guess they can't report much good detective stuff— like poisonings and stabbings and jewel heists, like in the big city. I mean, Pittsfield only has 9,327 people, not counting the farmers, of course, because they're not in the city limits.

Suzanna's OK, though. I didn't want to hurt her feelings. I decided to ask her, "What's it for this time?"

"You're probably right. It's no good for either of you. It's a Superkids Contest," she said, dangling the paper in front of me. "Changed your mind?"

"No joke? They're looking for a Superkid?" Quint asked. He snatched up one of his beer cans and balanced it on top of his head. "Then they're looking for me." He sat there without moving, like a statue. "Quentin A. Superkid, in person." He bowed low, and the can bounced off onto the grass.

"Do you have to play the saxophone or swallow swords or something like that?" I asked Suzanna.

"Try reading the rules," she said. "Page three." She threw me Dad's paper, popped a wheelie to show off, and sped away.

I rolled the rubber band off the paper and onto my wrist. We sat down on the old green park bench and I turned to page three.

14

"Here it is," I announced. " 'Superkids Contest, sponsored by the Pittsfield *Examiner*. Contest open to Pittsfield sixth-graders.' That's us, all right. 'Two winners will be chosen, one boy and one girl.' "

"Let me see that," Quint said, grabbing the paper. Then he read, in one breath, " 'Contestants must submit a one-page essay describing their hobby or special interest. The newspaper will select the finalists, and winners will be chosen by a vote of the Central School sixth-graders on Tuesday, May 18, after an assembly at which the finalists will speak.' " He put the paper down and started drumming on a can. "That could be running the hundred or tossing the Frisbee, almost anything."

Just then my little sister Julia came running across the street. Julia is five. She's got stubby brown pigtails, same color as my hair. Like me, she's little for her age. On her it's cute. On me it's shrimpy.

"Harvey!" she yelled. "Mom said you should push me on the swings." She gives orders a lot.

"Later," I told her. "I'm busy."

"I'll go home and tell," she said. She would, too. She's a tiger.

I went over and lifted her into a swing and did an underdog, running under and pushing her as high as I could. She was laughing like crazy.

Then it came to me. Just like that. I turned to Julia and said, "Hey, I've got my beer cans. I'm a Superkid."

"OK, Superkid," she yelled. "Push me higher."

"Say, Quint," I called, trying hard to keep myself from leaping into the air and clicking my heels together. "I'm going to enter. I've got my beer-can collection. I bet anything I can win with it."

"Not bad," he said, yawning at the idea. "Not good enough, but not totally bad."

"Listen, Quint," I told him, "I've got 798 cans, not counting the ones I just traded you. I've got more beer cans than anybody in this town. And I can get a lot more. I'll get a thousand, two thousand cans."

Quint wasn't listening to me at all. He went sprinting to the sandpile and did a running broad jump into the pit, taking the tower off some kid's sand castle. The kid hauled back and hit him with his shovel, but Quint didn't seem to notice. He sauntered back with a funny smile and leaned over close to my ear. "Magic," he whispered slow, like he was casting a spell or something. "I'll use magic."

I could see this thick yellow poison stuff steaming out of big black kettles, but Quint just reached in his jeans pocket and took out a beat-up deck of cards. He riffled them like a pro.

"Pick a card," he ordered, "any card." I did. It was the Queen of Diamonds. I put it back in the deck, and then, easy and slow, he made that Queen of Diamonds rise straight up and out of the middle of those cards until I could see her whole head.

"Fabulous," he sighed. "Fabulous."

I'd seen him fooling around like that before. It

was just tricks, though. "Sure, Quint," I told him. "It's good."

"It's better than good," he said. "It's great. What do I win?"

"What do *I* win, you mean," I answered, and Quint gave a big horse laugh. I read on. " 'Fifteen dollars in cash . . .' "

"Not enough," Quint cut in. "Keep going."

" '. . . and a ten-dollar gift certificate from the Hobby Hutch . . .' "

"The what? I never heard of it."

"Me neither," I told him. " 'The Hobby Hutch, Pittsfield's new hobby store, holding its grand opening Saturday.' And, listen, Quint—this is great. 'The Pittsfield *Examiner* will donate a trophy case to Central School.' And the first trophies in it are going to be twenty-inch Superkid cups—with the winners' *names* engraved on them."

Quint's face turned grim, and he stood up straight like he was leading the Pledge of Allegiance. "Harv," he said, "I've decided to win this contest." He grabbed his bike and tossed the cans into his basket. "Race you to the newspaper office. Bet I'm the first to sign up." And away he went.

"Push me again, Superkid," Julia yelled from the swing. "I died down. Push me again."

I reached for my cans and my skateboard and ran over to give Julia another swing. Then I followed fast after Quint.

It isn't a long way—six blocks or so—to the town

square where the newspaper office is. It's pretty fast going on a skateboard, too, if you don't hit Brown's shoe factory just when they're closing for the day. I skimmed down the sidewalk on Maple, swerving around most of the big cracks like on a slalom course, past the Methodist Church and the parsonage. I was just turning the corner at the shoe factory when I almost had a head-on with another kid on a skateboard.

"Trumble!" Eric Wagner shouted. "You're a menace on wheels." Eric's this guy in my class who showed me how to skateboard.

"Hey, look, I'm sorry," I told him. "Just had a crummy teacher."

"You're not so bad for a kid with two left legs," he said, and laughed. "Where you going?"

I didn't know whether to tell him or not. What if *everybody* entered the contest? Just what if? "Oh, down to the courthouse," I said. "Thought I'd skateboard around it. Give those old guys sitting on benches something to talk about." We've got this fancy hundred-year-old courthouse in the middle of the square, and every afternoon these same old men sit outside it and smoke and talk and watch the people go by. They don't like kids a whole lot. "I just thought it might be fun."

"I'd come with you, but I got a piano lesson. Listen, if you push off right at the bottom of the courthouse steps, it's downhill enough to give you a really good start. See you around."

18

I stuck the skateboard under my arm and walked the rest of the way. When I went in the newspaper office, I saw that Quint wasn't there. But his name was on the sheet the lady had me sign. Ours were the only names.

So what if Quint beat me to the sign-up? I was sure my beer cans were better than a curly lip and magic any old day.

2 · Avalanche

In bed that night I thought about all the kids who'd
see my name on a big gold trophy shining in its new
glass case. And they'd see my picture in the paper,
too. "Hey, that's Harvey," they'd yell. "I know Harvey Trumble. Everybody knows him. He's got more
beer cans than anybody in the world. I bet if he
stacked his collection up in two big piles, King Kong
would think they were the World Trade Center."
And I could see the old Goodyear blimp pulling
this long glowing sign through the night sky. *Harvey
Trumble, Harvey Trumble*, it flashed in red, white,
and blue lights. It was beautiful.

But then, when the pictures went away, I wondered
if I really did have enough cans. In the dark I could
hear my gerbils scuttling around in their cage and
spinning their ferris wheel. I could faintly make out
my beer cans in stacks around the room. They were
in alphabetical order—from Acme to Van Merritt.

I hadn't told Quint the truth, though. I didn't have
798 cans at all. It was closer to 600, and a lot of them
doubles. I don't even know why I told Quint I had
so many. Maybe the contest judges would count.
Maybe somebody would find out I was lying. If I

could make a lot of good trades and hustle around, I thought, everybody would realize it was a *serious* collection.

Still, even though it was midnight, I couldn't close my eyes. I needed a plan. Quint was so sure he would win. It was hard for me to be that sure. There was only one thing to do—fix myself a thick peanut-butter toast to help me think. My brain needed quick energy. I got up in the dark and tiptoed quietly across the cold floor.

Suddenly, I was flying. I was a rocket and I could see the stars to prove it. Somehow, I'd stepped down smack in the middle of my skateboard. It shot backwards, flung me forward, and slammed us both headfirst into four-foot stacks of beer cans. Those cans dominoed over and touched off more piles, which set off still more, and the avalanche just kept on going. A to V, all my cans were lying there scattered on the floor. Then, for maybe a whole minute, it was very, very quiet.

My big brother Peter snapped on the light. "You all right, Harvey?" he asked, his eyes half-open. There I was on the floor in my Green Bay Packers pajamas, with beer cans heaped around my feet, rubbing my head. As soon as he focused in on me, Peter closed his eyes, shook his head, and said very quiet and steady, "Harvey, why don't you grow up?" He staggered out, slamming the door so hard the cans clanged all over again, arranging themselves in new heaps.

Julia opened the door next, sniffling and stumbling in, dragging her stuffed owl Zachary by his wing. She did what she always does when she's mad and sleepy at the same time. She yowled like a siren. Then she started pounding me on the head with that crazy owl.

I was pulling myself up off the floor to swat her one, when my mom and dad appeared together, blinking at the light. At first they just stood there in their

nightclothes, staring. They took in the floor and then me, being beaten up with an owl by this runny-nosed kid.

"Oh, Harvey." Mom sighed, as though this was going to hurt her a lot more than it did me. She picked up Julia and Zachary and stumbled through the cans toward the door. "Harvey, Harvey," she went on, sounding like a record I'd heard before. "I think you should collect stamps. You can keep them in books, on shelves." As she left, I could hear her still talking through Julia's shrieks. "It's an excellent hobby, very quiet." She didn't shout, I guess, because she knew my father would.

He did, too. He blew his stack.

"Harvey Trumble," he roared, "you listen to me!" He kept pointing his finger at me to make sure I knew who he was talking to. "I've had just about enough of this nonsense. Those beer cans are leaving this house."

It's weird how things can strike you funny. I mean, beer cans leaving—it sounded crazy. I got this Technicolor picture in my head of all my cans sprouting legs, picking themselves up, snapping to attention, and leaving this house through the front door like some metal army. I was smart enough not to smile about it, though. The cans were just turning the corner and kicking their heels in the air when it occurred to me that he might be serious, and I realized that I'd turned the volume down. But when I switched back he was still talking loud enough to keep Julia awake. ". . . tell you right now about these cans." I hadn't missed much.

"One, they clutter up your room so it can't be properly cleaned." My father is very organized. He is always one-two-threeing things. "Two, they smell dreadful. Twelve-year-olds' bedrooms have no business smelling like a brewery." That wasn't really fair because I always washed my cans out. I really did. "Three, stacks of cans are painfully noisy when they hit the deck at midnight." From her room we could hear my sister give one last cry before plugging her mouth with her thumb. "Fourth, they make it look like I drink barrels of beer, which I don't. Fifth, and finally, I don't like them."

He reached down, picked up an Old Chicago can that had stopped at his bare toes, crunched it in half with one hand and tossed it back into the mess. My stomach churned. I figured I'd better argue, even though that hardly ever works with my dad.

"But Dad," I said. "Sir," I said, "I've been saving these cans for almost three years and I like them more than anything I've got. I do. I bet they're worth a thousand dollars easy. I ought to get twenty dollars alone for my Old Dutch cone top." I looked for it in the general direction of the O's, with no luck. I was glad that Old Chicago he'd crumpled was practically worthless. "It's here somewhere."

"Fine," replied my father, not really listening to

my grand totals. "Sell them. Or you can take them to the recycling center so they'll be put to good use again. But," he said pointing his finger in a grand sweep around my room, "I want them out of this house by Sunday night. Do you understand me?"

Reason hadn't worked. By this time I was begging. "Can't I keep the twenty-dollar ones at least, the really great ones like the Old Dutch conie and that Kato conie I got so cheap at the flea market?"

I looked around for it, but it had gone into hiding.

"Look, Harvey," he said, quieter. He was calming down. But he wasn't giving an inch. "It may say in those beer-can books of yours that you've got beer cans worth twenty dollars, but you can't tell me somebody'd pay you that. Do you know anybody who will?"

I didn't. He had me there. I didn't even know anybody who had twenty dollars to spend. So I didn't have a snappy Superman answer. I just wanted to keep my collection, all of it.

Dad closed the door quietly, leaving his midnight fury right there in the room with me and my banned cans. I decided to forget about the peanut-butter toast and get some sleep. So I waded through the clanking cans and climbed into my bed, an island in the middle of a rolling metal sea.

3 · The Gold Gazebo

We've got this gazebo in our backyard. It's a one-room summer house with lots of screens and fancy woodwork. On top its pointed green roof is a one-legged iron rooster that turns with the wind.

Early that Saturday morning after Dad banished my beer cans, I was sitting in the gazebo leafing through my beer-can book and eating a stack of peanut-butter toast. I was thinking about my poor cans and about the contest I couldn't win. No light bulbs were flashing over my head. My brain was stuck in neutral.

All of a sudden a terrific crash shook the roof of the gazebo and sent my plate of toast careening across the floor. Shingles from the roof zoomed down past the screen window. My teeth clanged together.

"It's a tornado!" I heard a kid scream.

"Tornado? Geez, it's a hurricane!" somebody else yelled, and the roof of the gazebo shook again. I leaped into the disaster drill squat they make us do at school—curled up with my arms over my head—clamped my eyes shut, and waited for a twister to lift me straight up by the hair.

"Spin, chicken, spin!" the first kid screamed, and the roof trembled again.

26

Chicken? Even if the tornado had hit a farm outside town, would a chicken still be spinning when it reached here? Anyway, who'd yell at it to keep going?

Suddenly I remembered it was a nice day. The sun was shining. But it didn't hurt to be cautious. So, carefully, I unwound myself and opened my eyes just far enough to see that the leaves on the big maple tree weren't even moving.

"Billy, help me! I'm falling!" The cry was coming from the gazebo roof.

"Grab hold of the edge, klutz," somebody else above me yelled. First I saw a pair of dirty sneakers dangle off the roof, and then the kid in them dropped into my mom's purple lilac bush. Something cracked. I hoped it was his leg and not the bush.

"What'd you have to do that for?" the kid on top yelled as he jumped off the roof. He landed right next to the first guy, who was rolling in the grass, moaning. It was Billy and Simon, the Terrible Two. They're eight, going on nine, and both of them live in the next block. They're always put in different classes because no teacher at Central School could handle both of them.

"Cut it out. I know you're faking," Billy said.

"I am not," groaned Simon. "I skinned my elbow and besides, I may also have a brain concussion."

"Not unless your brains are in your toes," said Billy. "You landed on your feet."

"Just what do you little vandals think you're doing?" I demanded. "My father will sue you." Dad was always *saying* he was going to sue somebody—people who didn't pay their bills at his drugstore or guys who delivered him junky hairbrushes with bristles that fell out. "If you hurt the roof, my dad—"

Simon tried to blow on his bleeding elbow. "*It's* not hurt. I am." Simon has a tangle of curly brown hair and thick glasses that make his eyes look big. And he really uses them. He gave me that look of total innocence he always gives grown-ups when he's in trouble. "We were just climbing your maple tree when we saw that weather vane. We never noticed it before."

"So we jumped on the roof and started spinning that chicken around," Billy said. Billy is a funny-looking kid. Four of his bottom teeth are out and his sandy blond hair is very, very short. His mother really sheared him the last time he got bubble gum stuck in it. Billy has more nerve than Simon, and he looked right at me and *smiled.* "You should have seen that bird go," he said, twirling himself around like a top. "Come on up, I'll show you." He started to climb back up.

"Get down here!" I boomed. "You guys leave, will you, while this place is still in one piece!" I yelled at them through the screen.

"This sure is a creepy place," Billy said, pushing open the screen door and walking right in. "Too dark for me."

"Good-bye," I said, trying to push him back out.

Simon stuck his head in the door and looked around. "What's all that lumber for?" he asked, slamming the door behind him.

"None of your business," I said. "Get lost, you guys."

"But we need some wood," Billy said.

"Well, you can't have this. Dad got it off a friend of his last summer, and he started to make this place into a playhouse for my sister."

"Not a bad idea," Simon said, pacing around. "But it's dark as the inside of a cat's stomach."

I flicked on the light in the peak of the ceiling. "Dad wired that up there," I told them.

"Why didn't he finish it?" Billy asked, pounding his fists on the boarded-up windows to see if they could take it. "It looks weird this way, half open and half shut."

"He just quit one day," I explained. "Julia kept complaining about the mosquitoes and spiders, and how spooky it gets, and how maybe there are ghosts out here and sharks."

"It sure is a waste," Billy said, picking up a loose board. "We could use this wood to build a tree house. We're good at building things."

"Forget it, guys," I said, opening the door to let them out. "It's time to move on to the next roof."

"Harvey, why do you want to get rid of us?" Billy said, tossing his ball in the air and not moving an inch toward the open door.

"Yeah," Simon said. "We're really great once you get to know us."

Great? Those two kids had reputations. They were pesty. Breaking windows or arms. Running over somebody's prize roses or riding through wet concrete. You were never sure what they'd do, so you had to be very careful. I kept the door open and waited.

"I'm not going to waste all day with you two, not with my big beer-can problem staring me in the face. If you're not out in five seconds I'm going to use some of that lumber on you."

"Beer cans?" breathed Billy. "You drink *beer*? That's against the law."

"We won't tell a soul," Simon said seriously. Billy crossed his heart and nodded.

"Knock it off, you guys," I told them. "For your information, I don't drink the beer. I collect the empty cans."

I could tell they didn't believe me. "You got to be kidding," Billy said. "What do you do that for?"

Since they asked, I closed the door and decided to tell them all about my collection. I'll tell *anybody* about it. I said I had a *thousand* cans. I'm not sure why I kept making the number bigger. I guess I figured that they were just little kids and didn't know much about numbers, so I rounded off to the nearest thousand. I told them about the midnight avalanche and the shouting match with my dad. I even told them about the contest.

"What's he want you to do with a thousand beer cans?" Simon asked. "Did he have any suggestions?"

"Sure, he had lots of suggestions." I'd been going over them in my head when Billy and Simon tornadoed me. "He said I could sell them for junk. But I don't *want* to sell them. I like them. Besides, they'll probably be worth enough to put me through college if I keep them long enough. I figure if I sell them to collectors I could get one or two thousand dollars for them, easy."

"A thousand dollars?"

"You're kidding. For *cans?*"

"No joke. I can prove it," I said. I picked up my trusty beer-can book and showed it to them. "Ever seen one of these?"

"No. We don't collect things," Billy said. "We're too busy."

"Look, I'll show you." I leafed through the pages of beer-can pictures. "See this Blackhawk can here? I've got that. See right after its name, it's got a 6/1? That means it's worth six ordinary cans—cans like this Hamm's—see?"

"Sure we see," Simon nodded. "How much is the ordinary guy—Hamm's—worth?"

I leafed through the book to show them how official it looked. "I don't want you guys to think I'm kidding you, so I'm going to show you where it's written right here in the book. Look. It says, 'The base can has a value of fifty cents.' Naturally, that's when it's in good shape. The Hamm's is a base can."

"You're trying to tell us that a regular old beer can is worth fifty cents?" Simon said. "Sure, sure." He didn't believe a word of it.

"No lie. I swear."

"You mean your Blackhawk can," Simon figured, "is worth six times fifty cents. *Three dollars?* Three dollars for one smelly old beer can? And you've got a thousand of them? Wow, you've got a mint in there."

"I know, I know. Now why don't you guys go away, so I can decide how to keep from losing my fortune." I flung open the door again, and since they didn't go outside, I did. I slammed the door and sat down on the step.

"Harv, I've got it," Simon called out. "This is what you do. First off, you get yourself lots of those huge black plastic bags. Put your cans inside. Then you move them all right out here into your gazebo."

It was such a dumb idea I couldn't believe it, but I went back inside and looked around anyway. "That wouldn't work," I told him. "They'd get soaked when it rains. They rust, you know."

"No, they wouldn't," Billy jumped in. He grabbed the board he'd been sitting on and ran over to a screened window to see if it fit. "All we have to do is close in the rest of these sides. We've already got a light up there that's bright enough for cans."

I had to admit the idea had possibilities. Tomorrow was the deadline for getting the cans out of the house, and the gazebo *was* out of the house. One problem, though. The rest of the sides had to be boarded up. I wasn't going to move my cans out into the rain, no sir. There was only one answer—child labor.

"You guys think you're pretty smart, don't you?" I paused to let the compliment sink in. "Well," I continued, "there's no way it could be fixed up by tomorrow."

"Come on, let us try." Simon was practically jumping up and down with excitement. All those kids wanted to do was build something and I had something that needed building. I was a little worried about them wrecking the place and themselves, but I had no choice. I decided I had to go all the way.

"Well, OK," I said, trying to look cool, "but no funny stuff."

"We can do it, Harv," Billy said, giving me that smile with the missing teeth. I shuddered. "We've even got some gold paint in our basement," he said. "It's left over from the Jaycees' Fourth of July float last year. My dad was chairman."

"Gold? A solid gold gazebo? That's really different," I said, trying to smile back. Actually, it didn't sound half bad.

"That'll make you the beer-can champion, all right," Billy said.

"Champion? I'll be king," I declared.

Simon giggled and scratched his head. "Well, Your Majesty," he said, climbing up the stack of boards. "You be king and we'll be knights."

"We'll need swords," Billy said. "And a catapult

for invaders. Maybe some pots of boiling oil."

Simon had reached the top of the lumber pile and was waving his arms, making proclamations. "Attention, serfs and peasants," he yelled. "I am Sir Simon, a knight most fearful and brave. All cheer." We did. Satisfied, he stopped proclaiming and sat down to blow on his elbow some more. "Sir Billy sounds silly," he went on. "You'll have to be Sir Bill or Sir William. Too bad there aren't any dragons for us to slay. You got any enemies, Harv?"

Somehow, the whole thing was sounding very good indeed. In fact, I could see my name shining across the sky again, like a meteor. "Listen to this, you knights," I told them grandly. "I'm going to win that contest, and I'm going to wear a gold crown when the newspaper takes my picture."

"Can we start building now?" Simon asked.

"Sure," I told him. "Well, maybe. I think I'll call Dad at the drugstore. He'll like it. I know he will. He's always trying to get me to do carpenter stuff. Then we can go get some hammers and nails. Simon, you come with me. Billy, you get the boards sorted out and we'll start to pound, all three of us. We'll turn this place into a real palace, a solid gold castle for me, Harvey Trumble, the Beer Can King."

"All hail," Simon said.

4 · The End
of the Rainbow

"Yipe!" Simon scored a direct thumb hit for about the tenth time. His fingernails were like magnets. We'd worked all morning and past lunch hitting nails, missing nails, bending them in half. Every time I said, "We'll never make it," Simon yelled, "We will," and Billy pounded faster. Finally, with the end in sight, Billy cut out to get the paint. Before too long Simon moaned, "I'm quitting," and tossed the hammer on the floor. "Billy's been gone half an hour. If he stopped to eat, I'll blast him." He slammed the door and sat down on the gazebo step.

Looking out across the yard I could see Billy pulling the wagon full of paint through the garden, squashing a row of yellow tulips.

"Good grief!" I yelled, running out to meet him. "Don't murder the flowers. Mom talks to those tulips. She read somewhere that flowers grow better if you talk nice to them. It won't work if their heads are off."

Billy turned and looked down at the flowers. "Hey, you guys, shape up." He squatted down to see what would happen. Then he turned to me. "What does she say to them?"

"She tells them they're looking good. She tells them they're going to grow up to be big and strong."

"Flowers won't listen to junk like that," Billy said, getting up and pulling the wagon across the grass. "It doesn't work with me, and I've got ears."

"Just in case," I told him, "use the sidewalk next time."

"How's it going?" Billy asked.

"We're all done," I told him. "I just pounded in the last board and Simon just finished off his thumb. There's still a crack or two between the slats, but we can always patch those up. Come on in and look around."

Billy stuck his head in and shuddered. "Geez, it's more like a dungeon now than a castle," he said. "Maybe we should put in a few torture instruments. How about a dentist's chair in the middle of the room?"

"What took you?" Simon asked. He sat on the step and watched his fingernail turn color.

"How'd you make out, Billy?" I asked. "You want to start painting now or later?"

"Maybe never," Billy said. "The paint's all wrong."

Simon was sucking his purple thumb. "Wass wong wiff it?" he asked.

There were lots of paint cans there in the wagon. I could see them. "Isn't there enough?"

"Sure, there's *enough*," he told us, pulling the wagon up in front of us. "I've got seven cans and three brushes. But it'll look crummy if we use it.

There was only one can of gold on the shelf. The rest are left over from different projects. Each one is a different color. Our castle won't be solid gold at all, or solid red or solid blue or solid green or even plain white. It'll look like an explosion in a paint factory."

"I hate it," I told him.

"No, listen, you guys, that's cool," Simon said, leaping up and forgetting his bum thumb. "Here's what we do. First off, we paint one wall gold and put Harvey's throne there."

"My what, where?" I hadn't said anything about a throne.

"A king's gotta have a throne," Simon explained. "At the A & P we can get some grapefruit crates. We'll make it out of those. They're not too strong, but they're wood, at least. We can paint the throne gold, too," Simon decided. I could see what they were doing. They were trying to take over my gazebo.

"I've *got* it!" Billy cut in. "Then we make these huge rainbows on the *other* walls. We'll use up all the rest of the paint on great big rainbows. I brought some paint along called Sunset Orange and Peppermint Pink."

"Neat," Simon said. "Perfect. And the beer cans . . . We'll stack the beer cans at the end of the rainbows. Get it? Get it, Harvey? They're the treasure. You get it, Harvey?"

"Sure, I *get* it," I told him. "Except I don't like

37

you little kids telling me what I'm going to do. Maybe I've got some other ideas for my castle and my throne. Maybe I don't want any Peppermint Pink rainbows."

"Why not?" Simon demanded. "Don't you think it'll be cool to have a heap of cans at the end of the rainbow? You said they were worth a lot, didn't you?"

"Look," Billy said in his mean-kid voice, "it's all the paint we've got in the basement. If you don't want it, I'll take it home." And he would have too, right back across the tulips. It sounded like a threat to me. Besides, I kind of liked the throne and the rainbow stuff.

"Don't panic," I told him. "It's OK. Look, it's gotta be one o'clock. You guys go eat lunch so Simon won't turn to bones and I'll meet you back here around three. My castle will be ready for its treasure tomorrow."

I made a big sweeping bow to them. They broke up, bowed back, and then galloped across the backyard, vaulting the tulips and the rosebushes. I heard Simon telling Billy how they were going to hang a sun from the ceiling. Over my dead body. Bossy kids.

Suddenly Julia came barreling out of the house. "Guess who got a letter?" she yelled.

"You," I guessed. "You finally got an answer from Santa Claus. Did he tell you why he didn't bring you that doll you saw on television?"

"He's too busy," she snapped. "Guess again."

"It's from the President. He wants Peter to be the first astronaut to play the piano in space."

38

"You're just teasing," she said, flapping the envelope back and forth. Then she stopped, stared at the boarded-up gazebo, and glared back at me. "How come you've been in my playhouse?" she demanded. "Who said you could do stuff to it?"

"Dad said," I told her. "I called him at the store. He said I could use your old playhouse because you don't."

"I do, too. You can't have it. It's mine."

"Look, Julia, we're going to fix it up like a castle and maybe you can be a princess or something." She didn't scream, so I figured the princess part did it. "Who got the letter? Was it me?"

She started dancing around again, waving it in the air. "Harvey got a letter," she sang. "Harvey got a letter. Scaredy Cat, Scaredy Cat, don't know where the letter's at." She hid it behind her.

I picked her up and took it away. She was getting ready to put on the old fountain-of-tears act, so I said, "Say, go look at our gazebo. This afternoon we're going to paint it with rainbows."

"Mother says you'd better eat now," she announced, wandering into my dark castle. I didn't need to worry about her. She was scared of the dark and I could hear the mosquitoes hum.

I tore the letter open. It was from the editor of the *Examiner*:

Dear Harvey,
    We have received your application for the

Pittsfield *Examiner*'s Superkids Contest. We are pleased that you are entering and would like you to send us, by Friday, May 7, an essay describing the hobby or special interest in which you excel.

When your essay is received, we will make an appointment with you to have a reporter come to your home to interview you and take pictures for the paper.

Finalists in the contest will be announced in the newspaper on Monday, May 17.

Good luck.

Sincerely,

George Adams

This contest was like an obstacle course. First, I gave them my application. Now the second jump was an essay. I guessed a lot of kids would drop out right away as soon as they had to write something, but not me. As I ate my chicken noodle soup, I read the letter again and tried to think of a few good things to say. I put three choice beer cans in front of me for inspiration, got out some notebook paper, and started to write:

COLLECTING BEER CANS

by Harvey Trumble

My hobby is collecting ~~empty~~ beer cans. I have ~~almost a thousand about eight hundred~~ hundreds of them in a ~~castle~~ gazebo in my back yard. I fixed up the gazebo like a castle and painted it gold inside with rainbows all around. I decided to put rainbows there because then the beer cans look like the treasure at the end of the rainbows. They are a ~~very big~~ really fantastic collection. They are worth a lot more than ~~two thousand~~ a thousand dollars. I learn about what they ~~████~~ are worth from reading beer can books.

This hobby is a ~~good~~ fabulous one because it is fun to collect cans and trade with other kids. Also it is good for the ecology because I clean up pollution when I pick up cans from the ground and out of the lake. This is a fantastic hobby and I excel in it.

I would like a reporter to see my beer can collection, my castle, and my gold throne.

Me, reporters, and a gold throne. Not bad. I stuck the essay in my pocket for copying over and ran as fast as I could out to the castle. Julia was sitting on the step, waiting.

"Can I see the rainbows?" she asked.

"Can you ever." I clicked the light on. "Just watch." I opened the paint cans with a screwdriver and set to work. I couldn't remember the way colors go in a rainbow, but I figured it didn't matter much since rainbows don't have Avocado Green and Peppermint Pink in them anyway. I made a small green half-circle, cleaned the brush off a little, dipped it in the Sunset Orange, and spread that on right above the green. Then I stepped back to take a look.

"It's beautiful," Julia said. "It's just beautiful. Harvey, do all rainbows drip?"

The orange paint was drooling down in little streams onto the green stripe. It looked rippled, like mountain brooks. It looked cool. But I decided to use less paint for the blue so the whole rainbow wouldn't ooze. Next, I sloshed on an enormous arc of red, and, above that, one of Peppermint Pink. By the time I got to the white stripe, I had to stand on the ladder. The smell of paint was so strong it almost made me sick. But the whole gazebo was changed. It was magnificent. You never saw a rainbow like it.

"Do another one," Julia begged. And I did. I kept on splashing up arches of wild, glorious color, and Julia kept on clapping.

5 · "Officer, Arrest Those Boys"

"Do you need another bag, Harvey?" Mom called up the stairs.

"Nope. The cans are all in sacks now. We'll take them out as soon as Quint shows up," I yelled back. "Only trouble here is the mice. Poor guys don't know where to go now I've pulled down their house. Shoo, mouse!" I shouted. My mom has this thing about mice. It all started when a couple of them got in the basement once and ate holes in this gingerbread house she was saving for Christmas.

"Harvey William Trumble, if you've brought another mouse into your room . . ."

"Just a joke, Mom," I told her. "Can't you take a joke?" Actually, I had once carried a mouse home from the dump in an old Falstaff can. He'd built a little grass nest in it, but I didn't know he was there till I got home. He and Mom were both glad when I took him back to his family.

The doorbell rang and it was Quint. I'd asked him to come over and help carry the cans out to my castle. I didn't need the help really, but I wanted to see his face when he took a look at the rainbows.

"Hey, I heard Eric Wagner's running," he told me right away.

"No kidding. What's he doing?" I asked him.

"Skateboarding. Remember his handstand push-ups going down Suicide Hill?" We took the steps two at a time up to my room. "You hear anything?" he asked me.

"Nope. I've been too busy getting my place ready. Haven't talked to anybody. What else do you know?"

"Well, Michael Holt might enter with his drums, and somebody said Matthew Marrinson was thinking about trying out with bird calls. I don't know about any others. You mail in your essay yet?"

"Yes. This morning," I told him. "How about you?"

"I mailed it on the way over. I got things all planned out. I'm going to have a fantastic block circus this Saturday in my backyard," he said, grabbing three cans from a big pile of doubles I had lying on my bed—some Schlitz, Lite, Budweisers—the kind I could collect a dozen of every day. He started juggling them high. "I'm going to be ringmaster, magician, and juggler. I'm a real pro." He missed one, so he let the others go crashing down with it to the floor. It didn't matter. I'd probably just toss them in the garbage anyway. "There'll be some other acts, too—dancing, clowns, a cat parade, stuff like that. Anyway, I told the paper that would be the best time for pictures."

"If it doesn't rain," I said, wondering if pictures of my beer cans would really look as good as pictures of his circus.

"It wouldn't dare," he said.

We carried the can-filled bags down the steps like two Santa Clauses on Christmas Eve.

"I'll give you boys some nice, warm brownies and a glass of milk when you're finished," Mom said, using her best bribe.

"Ho, ho, ho," Quint chortled as he shifted the weight to his other shoulder. Mom held up the brownies, still hot in the pan, and I could almost taste the chocolate.

The promise of food set us running across the backyard with our packs. I opened the door of the castle for Quint, snapped on the light, and stepped back so he could take a look. He gasped.

The rainbows were like huge hills of color waving around the room. It almost made you dizzy. At the end of one of them I'd already stacked a small pyramid of cans. They glittered in the light like the cars parked in used car lots. Swinging down from the light bulb was the big foil sun that Billy and Simon had made, and their grapefruit crate throne sat square in the middle of the gold wall across from the door. I walked over, sat down on the throne, and said, "You like it?"

I thought Quint was going to flip. "It looks like Oz," he said. "It really does."

"Dad put a lock on the door for me last night," I told him. "I was afraid somebody would just walk right in and rip off my cans. What do you think, though?"

46

"Never saw anything like it," he said, shaking his head. "What made you dream up all this stuff anyway? The rainbows and that crazy gold chair?"

"Well," I told him, "it's mostly because I've decided to be a Beer Can King. How's that for a title?" Quint was impressed. I could tell it. And that meant he was running scared. Boy, did I feel great. Grandly, I leaned back in my throne. The pine slats squeaked ominously. Figuring that falling on my bottom would put a quick end to my majesty, I jumped up fast.

Quint laughed and got that cocky winner's look again.

"Hey, I'm gonna stack the cans at the ends of all the rainbows," I told him, heading over to the one I'd finished.

"Like pots of gold?" He was still grinning, but I couldn't tell whether it was because he liked it or because he thought it was funny.

"G-e-r-o-n-i-m-o," yelled a voice that could only be Billy's. The roof shivered like I'd felt it shiver before and the light bulb in the ceiling flickered and went out. Standing there in the dark, Quint and I could hear him sing, "Round and round she goes and where she stops nobody knows . . ."

At least I didn't panic again and curl up on the floor. But before I could catch my breath to shout at Billy, Simon called him from way across the yard.

"Come on," he yelled. "Get back over here and help me drag this wagon. That weather vane is gonna fly off there if you're not careful."

The thud of Billy's jump to the ground shook us again in the darkness. We made our way to the door and looked out.

"What's going on?" Quint demanded.

Billy was roaring across the grass, yelling, "Stop! Stop it! Don't kill them. Listen, no more murder!"

Simon stopped, expecting, I guess, a land mine at least. He was right at the border of our garden.

Billy held his hand up like a traffic cop. "You gotta go around the flowers. You gotta use the sidewalk. Those flowers *talk* to Harvey's mom. Harvey was mad as a hornet at me for cutting some of their heads off the other day."

The wagon was piled high with junk. It really did need two people to keep it together. Billy broad-jumped over the flowers and they started off to the sidewalk.

"What's with Billy and Simon?" Quint asked again.

"They've been helping," I said as they raced toward us with their rolling heap. "They're not so bad. I've made them my knights."

As they pulled up in front of Quint and me, Simon said, "Wait'll you see it. Just wait'll you see. It was like magic finding this thing just when we needed it." He reached in the wagon and lifted out a fabulous breastplate of armor. It was real, solid, genuine, non-phony armor, not the stuff you make out of foil for Halloween. It was museum real.

"Come on, where'd you guys get that armor?" I demanded.

"In an alley."

"An alley?" Quint and I said together.

"It was just lying there with some rags and newspapers. Great, right?" Simon asked.

"Great, wrong," I told him. "Nobody's about to throw that thing away."

"Well, they did," Billy said. "It was there all by itself. Nobody was guarding it." He shined it with his shirtsleeve and put it back in the wagon.

"And, you guys, look at this," Simon said. "This is even better. Billy and me are gonna start can collecting, too. An old guy was throwing them out as garbage."

"In an alley, too?" I asked.

"Sure, an alley. What's wrong with alleys? The old man said he was cleaning his basement. He said he was moving to Florida and getting rid of junk like old clothes and bottles and beer cans," Simon explained. "We're going back to get some magazines and a washtub full of pop bottles. He told us we could have them."

Simon took the sack out and dumped at least twenty cans on the grass—*half of them cone-tops*! They could have been diamonds, they were so beautiful. I'd never seen them before in real life. They were like movie stars. You don't know for sure if they're real since you've only seen them in pictures. As far as I could tell, the conies were all from Minnesota. Four or five of them were Grain Belt. There was a Royal Bohemian, a Regal, and the rest were Rex. I knew the

49

books listed them all at around 20-to-1. Pure gold. They'd gotten some rusty old punch-tops, too, worth something, but nothing like those cone-tops.

"You guys hit it rich!" I shouted.

"Are they good ones?" Simon asked.

"They're great," I went on. "Why, *any* conies you find . . ."

"Look," Quint cut in, pushing me off to the side. "I bet Harv here will trade you some brand-new Schlitz and Pabst Blue Ribbon cans for those old cone-tops." I couldn't believe it. Quint was trying to get those cans for me. He must have known I'd give anything to get them. "Those punch-tops are rusty and old," he went on, "and really worth a lot. I bet he'd even give you some naval jelly to clean the rust off."

"*Naval* jelly?" Simon snickered. Billy bent over in dirty-joke-type giggles.

"Will you babies grow up," Quint told them. "Anyway, it's not belly-button navel. It's navy naval. They use this stuff in the navy to get rust off boats. But it works good for those valuable beer cans, too. Right, Harv?"

"Sure," I said, beginning to get a funny feeling inside that this wasn't a red-hot idea. I couldn't get over Quint helping me out. Why would he want to do that?

"Will you give us some of it?" Simon asked.

"You've got some to trade, don't you?" Quint asked, winking.

"Sure I do, but . . ."

"Sir Knights," Quint declared. "Your king will give you, absolutely free of charge, a bottle of naval jelly and a bag of—how many, Harv, twenty-five cans?" I nodded. "Twenty-five brand new assorted cans—Schlitz, Lite, Buds, Old Milwaukees—and you won't have to clean them up at all. You just give Harvey those ten cone-tops. That's better than two-to-one. Right, Harv?"

"Right," I echoed him. "Better than two-to-one. It's a great trade." I didn't say great for who.

"It's a deal, then," Quint said.

"Look," Simon asked me, "these cans you're trading us, what are they worth anyway?"

"What do you want me to do, get my book?" I asked, hoping he wouldn't say yes.

Simon shrugged his shoulders. "I guess not."

"Of course not," Quint said. "Harvey's OK. You just built a castle with him. You can trust him. Shake on it."

The way Quint talked it sounded like he was practicing to be a circus barker for Saturday. It was pure cotton candy and they were eating it up. Billy stuck out his hand and we shook. "Are the cans in the castle?" he asked.

"I left all the doubles upstairs," I said, not sure whether I should feel like a millionaire or a rat.

"Then Harv and me'll go get them," Quint announced. "You kids just sort out the punch-tops for yourselves. They're the ones that somebody's opened with a can opener. They don't make them like that anymore. They're antiques."

"Are they worth four-to-one?" Simon asked.

"At least," Quint told them. "Come on, you guys, Harvey and me'll be back in a couple of minutes."

As we walked to the house, I decided I couldn't do it. "I just can't cheat Billy and Simon like that," I told Quint.

"What do you mean?" he said. "They're just little kids. They'd rather have new cans. Listen, you need the cans and they don't. It's that simple. Don't worry about it because they'll never find out anyway. No way they're gonna find out. Besides, if you're gonna impress anybody with your collection, you're gonna need more cans than we carried outside today. You do what I tell you and maybe you'll make it to the finals."

I didn't say anything. He was still talking like the barkers at the circus, but he was right about the cans. I didn't have near enough to fill that big gazebo.

"Say," he said, suddenly, all excited, "did you notice how many of those cans had names about a king? Royal Bohemian and Regal and did you see the Rex —that means king in some language or other. It's like ESP or something." He grabbed my arm. "Can't you see," he said. "It's like those cans were meant for *you*, Harvey, the Beer Can King."

We each took a brownie on the way up. "No, listen," I told him, "I'd have to give them two or three hundred of those Pabst and Schlitz cans to make it an even trade and you know it. This'd make me more like Harvey, the Rip-Off Artist."

Upstairs, I gathered all the cheap doubles into a grocery bag, stuck in a bottle of naval jelly, and we walked down the stairs from my room, not at all like Santa Clauses.

"I can't do it," I told him.

"Then forget it," he said. "If you don't want to give me a run for my money, just forget it. But don't say I didn't try to help you. Just remember, those babies don't need 25-to-1 cans and you do. I'm going home and work on my circus. So long, sucker." He gave me the old skunk-smell lip curl and slammed the door behind him.

Maybe he was right. What's the harm, anyway, I thought. What Billy and Simon don't know won't hurt them. And those cans sure would help me.

I grabbed the whole plate of brownies to take outside. Billy and Simon were still in the yard, sorting. "Have a brownie," I told them. "Have two."

"We've decided we like collecting beer cans," Billy said. "Now that we've tried the alleys, we're going to go to the dump next."

"Here are your new ones," I said, "and the naval jelly." I spilled all the cans onto the grass and started stuffing the bag with my cone-tops. But those little guys looked so happy with those stupid, worthless cans that I decided, no matter what Quint said, I just couldn't go through with it. "Listen," I started. "This is just a big mistake—"

"There they are, officer. Those are the thieves!" a high shrill voice from the street cried out. A strange-looking old man with a deer-stalker's cap pulled down over his white hair came rushing toward us, a policeman following close behind. The old man stopped, grabbed the officer's arm, and glared at us from under his bushy white eyebrows. The policeman stared us down without a smile.

I thought I was going to die. The old man turned to the policeman and tugged on his arm. "I don't care how young they are. They broke the law and they should pay for it. Brats!" he shouted, letting the policeman go and moving in toward us. "Little boys didn't steal in my day. Arrest those pilfering boys, officer." And he shook his fist at us.

Mom came bursting out the back door. "Arrest *what* boys?" she demanded.

Nobody moved.

6 · Naval Jelly,
Absolutely Free

"Can I help you, sir? What are you doing in our back-yard?" Mom asked.

"My dear madam, I have reason to believe that there is stolen property in your backyard," the old man said, tugging at the brim of his Sherlock Holmes hat. He was wearing an old green sweater and around his waist a flowered apron, like he'd been interrupted doing the dishes. We all knew who he was. He'd retired here from Springfield to live with his sister over on Eubank Avenue, that street where the doctor, the funeral parlor owner, and Judge Melsheimer live. The old man always looked kind of fierce.

"Those two boys are the culprits," he said. He pointed at Billy and Simon slowly, one after the other.

"Are you absolutely sure, Mr. Watson?" the policeman asked him, looking at the two little kids and then at me. "Not the other one?"

"Of course, I'm sure," he growled. "I watched the whole crime from my kitchen window. Immediately, I grabbed my hat, called the police, scoured the neighborhood, and now we've tracked them down." He smiled triumphantly.

Billy jumped to his feet and ran over to the old man. "We thought you were throwing it away," he yelled. "It was right out there in the alley with the trash. It looked good, but it looked like garbage."

I knew it. I just knew it. Those cans were too good to be true. They'd lied to me about how they got them. They'd stolen them somehow from this old man's collection. I looked over at the bag of cans. As soon as he saw them, he would tell Billy and Simon how much they were worth. And then he would make me give them back.

"Officer," I pleaded. "They're just little kids. They didn't mean anything. The cans are all here." I turned to the old man, who was shifting back and forth, fuming. "They didn't know the cans were worth anything. They honestly thought you didn't want them."

Suddenly I felt glad to get rid of those cans. That would solve the problem completely. I wouldn't have to lie to Billy and Simon anymore. "Here, they're all yours." I reached down and handed him the bag of conies.

"What do I want with that rubbish? I never saw it before," he sputtered, throwing the sack of cans at me and wiping his hands off on the apron. "Do you think I'd call the police if those ragpickers stole a bag of beer cans? It's my *armor* I want. It's seventeenth century English and it is extremely valuable."

I couldn't believe it. He didn't want the cans. I just

sat right down on the grass and held onto the bag, hoping the old man was crazy as he looked and that he was going to change his mind.

"It's part of a collection, madam," he went on. "My father gave it to me as his father had given it to him." He directed this information at my mother, as though he thought she'd be the only one to understand.

"If it's worth so much," Simon said, "why did you leave it in back of your garage on a stack of rags and newspapers?"

"If you must know,"the old man growled, "I was all set up to clean it with naval jelly when I found there was none in the garage. So I went to the kitchen to look for more."

"Did you find it?" Billy asked.

"No, and I suppose I'll have to . . . Good grief, officer, I don't have to answer to this moppet. He has to answer to *me*."

The policeman looked at Simon and Billy and then back at the old man. "Mr. Watson," he said, clamping his hand kindly on the old man's shoulder, "if your armor was sitting on a pile of newspapers and rags in the alley, I think you can understand how the boys might have reasonably thought it was refuse."

"But they ran, officer. You should have seen them run."

"We always run," Billy told him.

"Besides, we were glad we'd found the armor for our castle," Simon added.

"We wanted to hurry and show Harvey," Billy told him. "He's the king, we're the knights, and over there is our castle." Billy pointed toward the gazebo.

"These children make no sense at all, officer," Mr. Watson said.

"They mean," Mom explained, "that they're sorry. But they want you to know that it's all just a mistake."

"Here's your armor," Simon said, lifting it very carefully out of the wagon. "It's got some dents and scratches on it, but we didn't do it, honest. No lie."

The old man took the armor from him, held it up for inspection, and then he put it on, holding it firmly against his sweater, the apron underneath it flaring out like a skirt. "Of course it's got dents and scratches, young man. It's seen *battle*. It's been struck with swords. That's where it's getting rusty, right here in the dents." He poked at the places to show us.

"You want some naval jelly?" Billy asked. "You can have this, absolutely free." He handed Mr. Watson the bottle I'd given him and Simon.

"It's great armor," Simon said to him. "But I sure don't see how knights wore whole suits of that heavy stuff. Can I try it on?"

"Not now, Simon," Mom said, standing between him and Mr. Watson. "This gentleman is just going home."

Mr. Watson shook his head. "I suppose you're right," he sighed. He started to leave, but whirled back around still clutching his armor, and said, "Next time though, young men, be careful what you take from alleys."

Simon dodged out from behind Mom and ran over to him. "Do we have to give the beer cans back to your neighbor who's moving to Florida?" he asked. "He said we could have them. No lie."

Mr. Watson took off his hat, fanned himself with it, and chuckled. "If George MacDonald said you can have his whole junk heap, you're welcome to it. He's a real keeper, that character is, hoarded stuff for years. His wife won't let him move any of it to Florida. Go ahead and keep the cans," he said. "You're probably doing him a big favor."

"Well, good-bye, Mr. Watson. Sorry about all that," Billy said.

"Good-bye, young men," Mr. Watson said with a little bow as he was leaving. "I will keep the naval jelly. I seem to be fresh out. Stop by for a visit and see the rest of my armor one of these days. I always like an appreciative audience. But just you stay away from my garage." And off he went. Maybe he wasn't such a bad guy after all.

The policeman put his hand on Simon's head. "Stay out of trouble now." He nodded to Mom and hurried off after Mr. Watson.

"Well, boys, are you all right now?" Mom asked.

"Sure, Mrs. Trumble, we're all right. I just wish he'd been throwing that armor away," Simon said.

"Come in if you get hungry," Mom called to us as she went back toward the house.

That left me all by myself with Billy and Simon. I didn't want to look at them. I knew Quint thought keeping the cans was a good idea. He was just trying to help me out. He's right, too, I thought. What do little kids know? They probably wouldn't even take care of those great cans. There was still time to tell them, but I couldn't do it.

"See you guys," I said, walking toward the gazebo. "I'm gonna stack cans in the castle now."

"Can we help you?" Billy asked.

"No, I want to do it," I told them. "Tomorrow you can help me put back the hammers and nails and stuff. And you can sweep up."

"Simon, do this. Billy, do that," Simon grumbled. "You want us to shine your shoes, too?" he asked.

"And brush your teeth?" Billy added. "What fun is clean-up?"

"Everything knights do for their kings isn't supposed to be fun," I explained. "Begone." I waved them away.

They gathered up their rusty punch-tops and the new beer cans, complaining all the time. And then they were gone, wagon, crummy cans, and all. Knights without armor.

7 · Taffy

Saturday was a gray, thunder-rumbling day, not at all perfect weather for Quint's block circus. Signs were taped up, anyway, on trees, lampposts, stop signs, everywhere:

CIRCUS TODAY
2 o'clock
TIGER PARADE – MAGIC – DANCING GIRLS
CLOWNS – JUGGLING – ACROBATS
at Quentin Calkins' house
1201 McCoy Street
Admission 10¢

I knew the reporter would come. The place would look great for pictures, with all the decorations, balloons, and stuff. I really wanted to go, even though Quint had been awful to me that week. I couldn't figure him out. During gym one day I told him about Mr. Watson and his armor and how he thought Billy and Simon had stolen it. I thought that would break him up, but he just said, "I bet you finally took their cans, didn't you."

"Yeah," I told him, "but I shouldn't have let you talk me into it."

He gave me a smirky laugh. "You're the one who did it, King Kan. I'm just a magician."

"Look, it was your idea!" I shouted. Boy, did he bug me. "You're not going to *tell* them?" I asked. And I could tell by that phony, fake smile that that was just what he was going to do. I pulled back my arm to let him have it.

"Trumble," the coach called. "Enough of that. Drop down and give me ten."

"All right. Tell them. They won't care," I told Quint and started the push-ups, which I hate. I knew they *would* care, though. I had to get to those kids somehow, before Quint did.

That's why I got to the circus early. Billy and Simon were sure to be there. Quint was using his driveway for a stage, so I sat down on the grass right at the edge of the pavement, so I'd be up front. The performers were mostly all in the garage getting ready and giggling. There were lots of little kids with clown faces painted on by their mothers and some twirlers from the Saturday morning beginner's class throwing batons up and dropping them on their heads.

I was sitting square in the middle of the front row, holding on tight to the box I'd brought with me. There was a lot of noise and yelling, so nobody noticed the squeaking and scratching inside the box.

When the popcorn kid walked by, I bought a bag for a dime, took out a big handful for me, and popped a couple of kernels into the box. I peeked inside and watched my two caramel-colored gerbils nibbling away. I had brought them as a peace offering, something to give Billy and Simon when I told them what the cans were really worth.

Lots of kids were at the circus, running around. I saw Billy and Simon. "Hey, sit down over here," I called to them. "I'll scoot over. Look, I've got something for you." I held up the box. They just stood there, not looking very friendly. "Where you been all morning?" I asked them.

"We went over to that new Hobby Hutch," Simon said slowly. "Quint told us there was something there we should see. He told us to price the beer cans there."

"He was right, too," Billy said, narrowing his eyes at me. "Mr. Grundle, the guy who owns the place, has got beer cans for sale. Not many, but enough. He's got a couple of conies like those we traded you. They cost twelve dollars each."

"It looks to us like we gave you a hundred twenty dollars worth of cans," Simon said. "Quint said you knew all the time. He said he didn't but you did."

"Yeah, Quint said the cans you gave us aren't worth a handful of beans," Billy went on. "We trusted you."

My stomach sank. The popcorn inside felt like Mexican jumping beans. I didn't know what to say. I was trapped.

"That Mr. Grundle sounds like a gyp to me," I tried. "He's asking too much. I don't know anybody

63

who'll pay that kind of money, do you?" I said, using my dad's line. "Anyway," I smiled, weakly, "don't worry about it. It's all for the good of the king." I kept hoping they still felt a little like loyal knights. I mean, what else could I say? I was *going* to tell them. But Quint got to them first.

Just then, Quint dashed out, waving a black construction paper top hat. Somebody yelled, "Down in

front," and Simon and Billy sat down next to me on the edge of the pavement.

"Ladies and gentlemen, children of all ages," Quint shouted. "The Quentin Calkins Circus is about to begin." A bunch of little clowns came somersaulting out. Some of them did cartwheels until their hats came off, even though they were rubber-banded under their chins. They were pretty good for first-graders.

The trees were beginning to blow, the sky was filling with more gray clouds, and in the distance you could see lightning. Quint didn't seem to notice. He led a round of applause for "those great little clowns," and then introduced, "The one, the only, Quentin Calkins McCoy Street feline pet parade." We could hear thunder rumble. Quint heard it, too. "Don't worry about it," he said. "It won't rain."

Just then the reporter from the *Examiner* arrived. She was wearing jeans and a short leather jacket and she didn't look much older than a high-school kid. You could tell she was a reporter, though, because she had a camera hung around her neck and she carried a big yellow writing pad.

As soon as Quint walked off and the kids with the cats started parading in, the reporter took Quint aside and started asking him questions and writing things down.

Billy glared at me. "Did you really know what those cans were worth?" he asked.

"You can have them back," I told him.

"Then you *did* know," he said, poking Simon, who shook his head.

"I brought you guys a present," I said, trying to pretend they hadn't found me out. I could hear the gerbils scuttling around inside as I held out the box.

"MEEEEEEEEEEEEEOWOWL!" We all turned at the howl of the cat parade. A little girl in a pink ballet dress was carrying a creamy Persian, its leash wrapped around her arm. Its eyes were wild and a birthday party bow had slipped down under its chin, like a weird pink beard.

Somebody had gotten a fat kid in a cowboy suit to show two cross-eyed Siamese wearing little paper saddles, but the kid looked like he was holding wild broncos. A huge tiger cat arched his back at them, giving a deep, snakelike hiss. The fat kid started to cry. An alley cat yowled.

Last of all was a girl pushing a baby buggy. Inside, climbing out of the covers, you could see this furry jet black creature dressed up in a frilly lace doll dress and bonnet. "Pretty kitty, pretty kitty," she kept saying to it, but no amount of "pretty kitty" was going to cool those cats down. They were mad.

Simon got up to go, tugging at Billy to come with him. "I don't like cats," he said, "and I don't like kings either. Let's get out of here."

"Simon," I called to him, "don't you guys be mad. I brought you both a present." I held up the box of gerbils.

"We don't want any presents." Billy shoved the box out of my hands so that it fell to the ground. He and Simon took off like a shot.

"WATCH OUT!" somebody screamed. I looked up and saw the Persian with the birthday bow dragging the pink ballet dancer across the grass. The cats had gone berserk.

"Where'd it come from?" somebody asked. Something brushed my hand. I looked down in the grass and saw a gerbil quivering in terror. The box was on its side and the top was off. I grabbed the poor, shaking animal, tucked him back inside his box, and started to look for the other one. I was sure he wouldn't run far.

"What is it, a rat?" somebody yelled. The cats were rioting. Owners were tugging on leashes, yelling and pulling as their cats meowed, hissed, and tug-of-warred to get away. That gerbil must have been crazy. He'd dashed straight through the legs of those cats.

Cats and kids scrambled everywhere, weaving leashes between other leashes and between legs until the driveway was a disaster area. The noise was something terrible.

Quint came running back, waving his arms. The gerbil had escaped, and all the cats seemed to have a different idea about which way he'd gone. Quint was right in the middle of it. Everybody was out of their seats laughing, trying to help, trying to unsnap leashes and tackle loose cats.

"Hey, you guys," Quint yelled. Nobody listened.

"Everybody sit down." Just then the rain started falling, big fat drops splatting on the ground. And on the
cats. The big black cat leaped angrily onto Quint's
shoulder, hissing. The reporter couldn't resist it. She
got her camera out and started snapping away. *Click*
went the camera. The kids were all running. The rain

fell harder. "Come back next Saturday and we'll do it again," Quint yelled.

Cats were everywhere. Two leashes wrapped around Quint's legs were tugged in opposite directions as kids tried to free their cats. *Click.* His feet slipped out from under him and he landed *pow* on his bottom like they do in silent movies. *Click* went the camera again.

"Here's that gerbil. I caught the gerbil," somebody called from the garage. A little kid in a wet clown suit held the gerbil up high over his head and asked, "Who's this belong to?" Nobody seemed to be paying much attention. I ran into the garage, holding tight to my box, rain dripping off the tip of my nose.

"Do you know whose gerbil this is?" the little clown asked me.

"He's mine. His name is Taffy," I told him, lifting up the lid and showing him the other gerbil. "This one's Toffee."

"Harvey Trumble did it," the kid yelled. "Hey, Quint. Harvey Trumble let the gerbil loose."

Quint ducked in the garage out of the rain. He was fuming. "I should have known it was you," he said. "You not only cheat little kids but you break up my circus. I'm gonna get you for this, Harvey Trumble!"

8 · The Royal Interview

I was sitting on my throne, waiting, when somebody knocked on the gazebo door. It was too early for the reporter, so it had to be Quint and his gang or maybe Billy and Simon with theirs, come over to bloody my nose and cauliflower my ears. I got up and looked for someplace to hide, but unless I could genie myself into a beer can there was no place to go. The knock got louder and faster.

"Harvey, Harv. You in there?" It was my brother Peter. Good old Pete.

"Enter, slave," I commanded. "Enter my castle."

"Your Majesty," he said, swinging the door open. "Your obedient servant here." He looked around the room, tracing the rainbows with his eyes. "The old gazebo will never be the same. How're you doing with all this stuff?" he asked.

"Awful," I admitted. "Being a king is great, but I'm messing everything up. Billy and Simon are mad at me because I gave them a lousy trade trying to beef up my collection. And Quint's mad. I ruined his circus yesterday." Everything, everything was wrong.

"I thought it got rained out."

"Well, I didn't make the rain, but everything else

was my fault. One of my gerbils got loose—accidentally, I swear—and it totaled his cat parade. Quint said he'd get me for it, too." Peter was wandering around moving cans. It didn't look like he was listening. "What do you think he'll do?" I asked Pete as I followed him, putting the cans back the way they were.

He walked over to the throne. The whole gazebo looked smaller when he was in it. He could reach up, if he wanted to, and change the lightbulb in the peak. He didn't answer my question. "Your old buddy Eric Wagner called," he told me. "He said Quint had called him. Eric said to tell you *he* knew you hadn't done anything on purpose, but that you better watch out for Quint. He's planning trouble for you."

"You mean he . . ."

"Also," he went on, "Matthew Marrinson called to ask if you were interested in trading him a Falstaff Draft for a Dixie and a Jax. His folks just brought them back from New Orleans. He said he'd decided not to enter the contest because he doesn't like to make speeches."

"That's too bad," I started, "I . . ."

"That's not all," Peter broke in. "Quint called *him*, too. Matthew wants you to know he's not going to join Quint against you."

"Against me? Did those guys say what Quint wanted them to do?" I asked him.

"Some sort of organized madness directed at you.

71

They didn't say. I didn't ask. They're your friends. Call them back and find out. Or just let it be a surprise."

He started to sit down on my throne, and was hovering about three inches over the cushion when I yelped, "Peter, don't. That throne's made of crates. You'll pulverize it."

Peter straightened up, looked for another place to sit, and, not finding one, started toward the door. "If you need any help, Harv, let me know. Though I'll admit I've never been a king's bodyguard before."

As he opened the door to take a giant step out, Julia came skipping in, beaming. "There's a lady wants to see you," she said. "She's got a camera."

"It's the reporter," I told her. "She's gonna take my picture for the paper."

Julia twirled around a few times on her toes. "Can I dress up like a princess and get my picture taken, too?" she asked.

"No, you can't," I told her, looking around to see if everything was all shaped up. "I'm the king of this place. Where is she?"

"Outside." She peeked out the door. "Talking to Peter." She turned and looked me over. "You don't look like a king," she said. "You oughta have on your crown. Where is it?"

Julia and I'd made a crown together out of old gold wrapping paper, but I thought it looked too dumb. I'd just stuck it on top of the throne. Julia saw me glance over at it and went dashing over to lift it off. "Put this on," she ordered. "It's beautiful."

I clamped the crown on my head as she dashed out the door, announcing, "My brother the king is inside the castle. That makes me a princess, you know."

The reporter patted Julia on the head and stepped in the door. She was the one who had talked to Quint. She looked around the dimly lighted gazebo. Then she saw the royal me. If she remembered me from the circus she didn't show it.

"I'm Harvey Trumble, the Beer Can King," I said, holding out my right hand and steadying my crown with my left. "I'm Karen Gray, the reporter," she said, smiling and shaking my hand. I asked her if she wanted to sit down. Since the throne was the only possible place, she said no thanks and started touring the cans.

"Where'd they all come from?" she asked me, getting her pad and pencil ready.

"Lots of places," I told her. "My uncle in Springfield got me started. He'd saved about a hundred cans and he gave them to me for my birthday three years ago. They're all mixed in with the others now because I've got them in alphabetical order." I started to lead her over to the A's, but I noticed she was writing like crazy. It scared me to watch her put my words on paper, so I stopped talking.

She stopped writing and looked up. "And you built up from there?" she said. I nodded yes. "How?" she

73

asked. The pencil was on the paper there, ready to go. "On vacations," I said.

"On vacations," she wrote.

"Is that all?" she asked me.

"Not really," I told her. She didn't write that one down.

"You don't sound much like a king," she said, looking at my dumb crown and then at all the crazy rainbows. She started to put her pencil back in her big leather purse.

"But I really am a king," I said, pleading. "I'll tell you all about my cans. They're fantastic. Take this Rex conie, for instance," and I kept her pencil going for twenty minutes easy. I told her about cleaning up rusty cans with steel wool. I told her how to straighten out a dented can by dropping a lighted firecracker into it.

I told her about finding cans in gas station trash barrels and in alleys and dumps. I told her about snaking around on the bottom of lakes near picnic places. I told her about trades and about flea markets, about conies and punch-tops. Every time she stopped writing I told her how great I was. I even told her about my trusty knights once when I couldn't think of anything else to say. It was great being a king with an audience. I could have talked all day. I was just taking a breath to go on when she started to take out her camera.

"Hold up," she said. "I've got enough for three articles. What I need now is a picture."

I grabbed the nearest can, an old Hirshvogel quart conie, sat down on the throne, and smiled as big as I could.

Click went the camera.

"Hold the beer can up in front of you. It looks kind of old, but I guess it'll do. Up higher." *Click.* "OK, now hold the can near your face. Smile." *Click.* "I guess that's it."

"Anything else you want to know?" I asked her.

She laughed. "You know, I thought you weren't

going to talk at all there at first," she said, "but you told me all I need to know about beer cans. Thanks."

"Har-vey," Julia yelled from outside in the yard. "Harvey, you've gotta come here. Some kids are out here."

"Good old Julia," I said. "She's gotten a batch of her little friends to come and see me in my crown."

"Harvey," she yelled again. "They want to see you."

I was still seeing stars from the flashbulbs when I flung open the gazebo door. The gold paper crown sat on my head. I smiled my best, my kingliest smile— for about three seconds.

Splat. Right in the forehead it got me. Egg oozed down my eyebrows and dripped off my chin. My crown fell to the ground. *Splat*. In my hair. I wiped my eyes free of the sticky goo and saw Billy and Simon standing there, eggs in hand.

Simon was winding up.

"What's going on out . . ." *Splat*. Karen Gray got one, too.

"You guys didn't tell me you were gonna do that." Julia was crying. "That's not fair."

"Geez, I hit some lady!" Simon yelled. He and Billy dropped their eggs and took off across the grass, with me running wildly after them. They jumped over the flowers.

"Hey, King Kan," somebody called. I looked out toward the street and there was Quint, standing on the sidewalk, laughing his head off.

"Some king!" he roared. He looked around, smirking, to see if any other kids were there to enjoy the mess. But I watched his face change plenty fast as his eyes reached the gazebo. The reporter was standing there, egg all over her face. She didn't see Quint. Her eyes were glued shut. But he sure saw her, and I bet he beat his own record running the hundred.

I tried running after him, but the faster I ran, the drier the egg got. My face was stuck. I couldn't move it.

When I got back, my mom was in the yard with a wet towel for the reporter. Mom was telling her what she thought of Billy and Simon. "Those boys," she was saying. "Last week, I saw them jumping up and down on the roof of the gazebo. Then, a few days later, they took somebody's valuable armor—they *said* by mistake. And now this. Well, I can't tell you how sorry I am."

Karen Gray wiped her face mostly clean with the wet towel. Then she smiled at Mom and laughed out loud when she looked me over. "You know," she said, "I thought covering this contest was going to be a real bore. But it's been incredible. Incredible," she said again, shaking her head. She was still smiling when she waved good-bye with her spattered yellow pad.

I went inside the house, filled the bathroom sink with water, and stuck my head in. As the warm water

77

began to loosen my face, I shifted it from smile to frown and back. I puckered, blew a bubble or two, and lifted my head out of the eggy water for air. I looked in the mirror. It was pretty bad. That Billy had a good pitching arm, I'll give him that. He'd hit me square in the middle of my forehead. The hair hanging down over my eyes was all matted together

and bits of egg-shell stuck in it like snowflakes. I looked more like the king's fool than the king.

Peter came in to look over the damage. "I'm not a very good bodyguard," he said. "I didn't hear a thing. You OK?"

"I'm OK. Just yucky," I told him as I soaped off the egg streams.

"Ever hear of the French Revolution?" he asked me.

"American, yes. French, no," I told him. "Don't try that high-school stuff on me."

"There was this king," he said.

"Oh, come on," I groaned. He was going to preach at me. I could tell it.

"No kidding," he said. "This kind of stuff happens to kings all the time. They get to feeling their power. They rob the peasants and the peasants get mad and fight back."

"Billy and Simon aren't peasants," I told him, as I toweled my head dry.

"I didn't say they were," he said. "Anyway, one of the reasons for this French Revolution was the king. Louis the Sixteenth. You know what they did to him?"

"I'd hate to guess."

"Guess."

"They egged him."

"Close, close," he said. "They cut off his head." He bent over the sink and chopped at his neck with the side of his hand. "Sliced it off, *thunk!*" he said, letting his head go limp.

"Oh, cut it out." I snapped the towel at him while he was bent over. He was making me mad. "Nobody's going to cut off my head for ripping off a couple of little kids."

"Aha! You admit it," he said, straightening up. "You didn't just make a good trade. You ripped them off. *That* is the downfall of kings, kid."

"Yeah, well, it just happened. Now I don't know what to do about it."

"Simple," he said. "Give them back the cans."

"Sure, simple." I wound the towel around my head like a turban. "I'll think about it."

"I would if I were you," Peter said as he left me standing there. "If you don't give those cans back pretty soon, Your Majesty," he said, "I'd bet the revolution has just begun."

9 · The Monster and the Magician

All the kids at school Monday were laughing about how I'd been egg-bombed by those two third-graders. I didn't see Billy and Simon all week, though. Oh, I saw them all right, but when they saw me they ran like crazy. I guess they thought I was really sore. But the more I thought about it, the more I was sure I would have egged the guy who cheated me out of those cans.

On Friday, Quint came up to me in the hall with two of his friends hanging around behind him. "Look," he said. "I'm gonna have another circus tomorrow and I've got some guys who are gonna be there looking for you. Not just Billy and Simon this time, either. I've got more." The warning bell rang and everybody started slamming lockers and running toward their rooms.

"I don't care about your old circus," I said.

"You better not come, that's all," he told me. "You better not." And he ran off down the hall.

I decided right then to go, but I wasn't exactly sure how. I couldn't see getting together a gang of guys to force my way in. I didn't want to ruin the dumb circus again. Anyway, Julia was going to be in it this

81

time, wearing her new tutu, and she'd kill me if I botched it up for her. There had to be some secret way to go.

Julia woke me up on Saturday morning. "Mom's gone shopping," she said. "You've got to fix your own breakfast. And we're out of peanut butter." She handed me a sheet of paper that had been printed on some kid's printing press.

QUENTIN CALKINS CIRCUS
FABULOUS JUGGLING AND MAGIC SHOW
today at 2
Absolutely free to kids who paid last week
Absolutely one dime to kids who didn't
NO CAT PARADe

Julia said a couple of girls were handing out the ads on Lake Street.

"You gonna come and see me do the splits?" Julia asked.

"I don't know," I told her. "Go away and let me wake up." I got up, washed my face awake and tried to start thinking about disguises.

First, I decided on clown makeup. But I figured somebody would be sure to find out it was me under the paint. Then I wandered into Pete's room to look at his mask collection. Most of them were stashed away in his closet, but three of them were sitting on stands on his dresser. There was his Richard Nixon mask. It was a great one. It really was. But it wouldn't do. I used it once for Halloween and people kept stopping me and asking me questions. People want to talk to Richard Nixon. The ape mask was pretty good, but it was new last year, so I decided to wear Pete's old monster mask. It was horrible, green-gray and yellow soft rubber, with pink scars and two gruesome fangs. Nobody would even see my hair because the mask covered my whole head. Next to it on the dresser were ugly, warty monster hands with long jagged green claws. They were perfect. Nobody would even notice me, I would look so circus in a getup like that. Nobody was likely to come up and ask a monster questions, either.

But the beer cans were another problem. Somehow, I had to get those conies back to Billy and Simon. Those ten cans were driving me batty. I just wasn't sure how to return them. Should I stack them up on one of their porches and let it go at that? Should I wrap them up like presents and drop them down their chimneys? Maybe I could just walk right up and say something sincere like, "Here you are, my friends. I am deeply, deeply sorry. I have decided I was wrong wrong and you were right right and you can keep your stupid cans."

Actually, I tried out several speeches, but I could always imagine Billy shouting out something like, "Couldn't take the eggs, could you? What's the mat-

ter, scared?" when it really wasn't that at all. I just
felt guilty. I tried to tell myself that we *did* shake on
the trade, after all. I *did* give them some of my cans
for theirs. It wasn't as if I stole them. But I couldn't
talk myself into it. I'd given them a crummy trade
and that was that.

I went out to the gazebo, unlocked the door, turned
on the light, and looked around. It was still a great
castle. Those ten beautiful conies were lined up on
a stack of boards we'd painted with the leftover gold.
I'd buffed off the bad rust with steel wool, shined
them up with naval jelly, and coated them with wax,
so they looked first-rate.

I wrapped each can carefully in a sheet of news-
paper and put them all in a big grocery bag. I figured
I'd think of some way to deliver them to Billy and
Simon.

At two o'clock I left for Quint's circus with my
big bag of cans. My hands and face were all sweaty
inside the monster getup and my hair was sticking to
my forehead, but I figured if Pete could take it on
Halloween, I could stand it for an hour or so.

On a lamppost down the street there was a poster
that said Eric Wagner was going to give a skateboard
show at four o'clock on Suicide Hill. That meant
Karen Gray would be at it again, taking pictures
and asking questions. After the circus I'd go over
and watch him. Suicide Hill's no joke. It's really
steep, heading down toward the creek and the band-

shell in the park. But Eric's good . . . wears elbow and knee pads both. He sure makes that board work for him.

Wandering into Quint's driveway, I passed the kid who was collecting dimes, waved my green claws at her, and walked on in. She waved back and giggled at me.

The little clowns were already somersaulting. I had this creepy feeling that I'd done all this before and that it wasn't going to be any fun at all. Billy and Simon were in front with a gang of kids, eating popcorn and shouting to a tiny clown in a pointed hat, "Stand on your point, pencil head."

I leaned up against the tree, back from the crowd, and put the bag of cans down next to me. A little kid selling popcorn edged cautiously over to me. I bought some from him with the dime I had in my paw. I'd brought it along just in case I had to pay to get in.

It's very hard to get popcorn out of a bag when you're wearing warty rubber hands and it's even harder to fit it in the mouth slit of a mask. I tried. I even got some inside, but the mouth of the mask was about an inch below my chin. The popcorn just kept slipping out of the mask and into my shirt. It was useless.

Giving up, I looked over to see Quint running in to announce, "And now, ladies and gentlemen, it's time for MAGIC!" He flung out his hands and, suddenly, a very long black cane with a white tip appeared in one of them. Just like that. It really wasn't there before. He twirled it around, stuck it under his arm, and bowed. The kids all clapped. It was pretty good. I clapped, too.

Next, Quint called up one of Julia's friends, a little kid in a blue ballet dress and a pink feather thing in her hair. She was pretty nervous with everybody looking at her, but she managed to crumble a soda cracker Quint gave her into a metal pan, just like he asked her to. Then he handed her a jack of diamonds and asked her to tear it in half.

"*Tear* it?" she asked. She couldn't believe he really wanted her to.

"Sure, tear it in half," he said.

She tore it in four pieces. He took the torn-up card and tossed it in the pan with the cracker crumbs, put a lid on the pan and waved his cane around going "Presto-chango" and "Hocus pocus dominocus." He told her to close her eyes and blow her magic breath on the pan. She did it, and you could tell she believed she was really working a spell, too. She opened her eyes. Quint lifted the lid off, and—you're not going to believe this—but right there where the crackers and the torn jack had been, there was this big box of Cracker Jacks.

"Cracker—Jacks!" Quint said. "Get it?" Everybody had already gotten it. And they clapped a lot. I clapped with my rubber mitts. I was feeling kind of hot inside, but this was fun. I was glad I'd come.

Then Quint held his hands up to quiet everybody and said, "I need another helper."

All the kids in front were waving their hands in the air, screaming, "Me! Me! My turn!" Quint roamed his eyes over the group in front of him. He glanced over at me, leaning against the tree, looked away, and then looked quickly back again.

"I want the monster," he said slowly.

All the kids stopped yelling, "Me! Me!" and turned around to see what he was talking about. They must have figured this was all set up ahead of time because a couple of guys in clown suits started to shout, "We want the monster."

I shook my head no.

Quint nodded his head yes, and everybody laughed. I couldn't tell if he knew who I was or not. "This trick is perfect for the monster," he said with a mean grin. And I decided he knew. Somehow, he could tell.

Everybody started chanting, "We want the *mon*-ster. We want the *mon*-ster." Some little kids ran up and started pushing at the backs of my knees, moving me forward. I kept shaking my head no and they kept yelling, "*Mon*-ster."

The cans! When I turned back to get them they were almost out of reach. I lunged back, grabbed the sack, and let myself be swept along in a tide of little kids, right up to Quint.

When everybody had settled down, Quint held up

an old *Examiner* with a picture of a burning grocery store on the front page.

"Now, everybody remember this page," he said. "Find something on it you'll recognize when you see it again." Then he turned to me. "All I want you to do is tear this newspaper in half. Can you tear paper absolutely straight, monster?"

I shook my head no, wiggling my rubber claws. The crowd giggled.

"Then I'll do it myself," he said. He held the newspaper up high and tore it in half the long way. Next he tore each of those pieces into two strips. Because I was standing so close, I could step a little behind him. I could see another newspaper. It was folded and pasted on the back of one of the torn strips. Seeing that, it wasn't hard to figure out how the trick was done. He was going to fold up the pieces and open up that other paper. It would look like the first one had just magicked itself back together.

"This is some rip-off, isn't it?" Quint said, getting another laugh, as he tore the newspaper into more pieces.

Rip-off? That's why he called me up here. That's why he said it would be a good trick for the monster. He was going to say something about me and that other rip-off.

In the front row Billy and Simon were laughing. Simon was pointing at the newspaper and talking all excited about something. I tried to listen. I could hear Simon say he'd figured out how the trick worked. Maybe he'd seen the folded-up paper, too.

I looked back at Quint just as he was presto- chango-ing. He folded up the torn pieces into a small package and suddenly, *flip,* there was one whole newspaper with a picture of a burning grocery store on the front page.

Everybody yelled and shouted and I could hear Simon saying, "See, see, I told you so."

Quint got everybody quiet and started off with, "That was some rip-off. Didn't I tell you? And now," he said, "for yet another rip-off." I could feel his hand grab the back of my mask. "Hold still," he said, quietly. He was getting ready to tear it off with everybody watching.

I had to do something. I couldn't run or disappear. Fighting him would break up the circus again. The kids were all watching close. They thought it was just part of the act, The Monster and the Magician. I decided to keep the act going.

Just as Quint was yanking the mask up in back, I raised my claws up high and roared. It was a ferocious, monster roar—loud, but muffled and mysterious, since the mask kept part of it echoing inside. Everybody stopped talking. Quint dropped his hand and stepped back.

"A prize," I roared. "I have a prize." I held up the beer-can bag and swung it back and forth in front of them. "The Monster will give a rich prize to the

first person who can tell how the Magician performed
his fantastic newspaper trick."

Simon jumped to his feet. "I can!" he shouted. A
lot of other kids shouted, "Me," but I pointed a claw
at Simon. "I can," he said again. "He had another
newspaper folded up and pasted on the back! Right?"

"You're right," I growled as loud as I could. "You've guessed the Magician's deepest hidden secret." I bowed and pointed to Quint, who didn't bow, and everybody cheered. This, I decided, was the time to leave. The kids were yelling, "*mon*-ster, *mon*-ster," as I waved good-bye. I tossed the bag of cans to Simon, yelled, "The Monster congratulates you on your all-seeing eyes," and growled off down the driveway. Quint was standing there with his mouth open, not knowing what to do. I guess the only thing he could do was go on with the next act, Julia and her friends in tutus doing the splits, maybe.

Sweat had collected in my ears and my hair was as wet as if I'd been swimming. When I took off the mask a block or so away I must have looked like an endangered seal. I sure felt like one. I had to laugh, though. What if Quint had torn off the mask and it was some other kid, not me at all? I whistled as I walked along.

"Harvey?" a voice said. I turned around. It was Suzanna, tooling along on her unicycle. "You all right?" she asked. "You look funny."

"I'm great," I told her. "I'm just sweating from this monster mask." I held it up for her to see and she looked at me as though I was absolutely off my rocker.

"Hey, Harvey! Harv!" Suzanna and I both turned this time. Billy and Simon were running down the street, shouting.

91

"You were really great, Harv," Billy yelled. "You really were funny."

"We didn't know it was you until we opened the bag. No lie. But you didn't need to give back the beer cans," Simon said. "We were just mad that you traded like that." He held out the bag. "We didn't really want the cans."

"I don't want them either," I told them, putting my hands behind my back. "They're yours. You found them. Every time I see them they give me the creeps."

"Take them," Simon said.

"I can't," I said again.

"Beer cans?" Suzanna asked, getting off her unicycle. "Good ones?"

"Conies," I told her, figuring she wouldn't have any idea what I was saying.

"You're kidding," she said. "I'll take them if neither of you wants them."

"What for?" Simon asked.

"What do you mean, what for?" Suzanna asked. "For collecting, of course. What else would you do with conies?"

"You've got a collection?" I asked her, wondering if she was putting me on.

"Sure, I've got a collection," she said. "Well, really, my dad and I have this collection. He drives a truck and he picks them up from all over the country. And when he's home sometimes we go out looking for cans. Then we blast out the dents or fill them with water and freeze them out. We clean and buff and wax them, you know, stuff like that. We've got one thousand, one hundred and forty-eight cans from all over, and we're going to a collectors' convention this summer while Dad's on vacation."

I crumpled the mask up and stuck it in my pocket. "A thousand one hundred forty-eight? You really mean it?" I asked her. "Lots of doubles?"

"Not counting doubles," Suzanna said. "Dad says it's not fair to count doubles." I was beginning to sweat as bad as when I had the mask on. I rubbed the drops off my forehead with my sleeve.

"Look, I know what these cans are worth," Suzanna said. "Nobody's going to give them away." She laughed.

"It's OK with us," Simon said.

"Take them," I told her. "You and your dad can have them." They had a *lot* more than me. They made my collection look like zero, zilch.

"Look," Suzanna said, "my dad won't be back in town until Tuesday, but I'll take these home and see what he says. Thanks a lot." She hopped back on her unicycle, circling around a couple of times before she rode off, holding the bag of conies in one hand and waving good-bye with the other.

A thousand one hundred and forty-eight cans! Some Beer Can King I was turning out to be.

10 · The Boy
Who Would Be King

I had tons of homework Monday. I was sitting in front of the TV watching a game show and trying to figure out how you're supposed to divide decimals when Julia called me.

"Harvey," she yelled. "Har-vey, come here."

I didn't answer. If I came every time Julia called me, that's all I'd have time to do.

"Harvey," she called again. "Come here!"

On the other hand, if I didn't answer, she'd keep calling me forever.

"I'm busy," I said, thinking that might do it. I tried to remember whether you move the decimal point right or left.

"Harvey!" She was mad now. "Don't you *care* that your picture's in the paper?"

That did it. I got downstairs by the bannister in three seconds flat. She didn't even try to hide the paper from me. I grabbed it and lay back on the living-room sofa to soak in the glory.

"SUPERKIDS FINALISTS," the headline said. Underneath were six pictures and mine was one of them. The girls were Anne Wilson, this kid who swims like a salmon, Debby Goldsmith, who plays a mean flute, and Suzanna Brooks. There was a really great photo of her eating a hamburger while she rode on her unicycle.

The boys were Quint, Eric Wagner, and Me! Quint's picture was the funniest. It was the one Karen Gray took when the cats were starting to tie knots around his legs. The black cat in a dress was clinging to his shoulder and he looked like his face was about to slide off. Under the picture in big letters it said, "The Presto Chango Kid." I skimmed the article, which told mostly how hard he practiced his magic and how the little children of the neighborhood adored him for putting on magic shows for them.

Eric Wagner's picture was a good one. He was standing on his head on his skateboard, smiling. You had to turn the picture upside down to see the smile. From the way he looked, you knew he could skateboard down roller-coaster tracks if he wanted to. Under his picture it said, "Down the Hill Upside Down."

Then there was me. It was a dumb picture. My old Hirshvogel can was stuck out toward the camera in perfect focus. Behind it, kind of hazy in the background, was me in my crown. The gold wrapping had peeled down from its points and you could see the cardboard underneath as plain as day. I had a silly grin on my face, too. It wasn't the picture I'd thought it would be. One thing it *didn't* look was grand and noble. But under the photo was the real clincher, like a big put-down. It said, "The Boy Who Would Be King."

I didn't want to read any farther, but I couldn't help myself. "Harvey Trumble," it said, "wants to be a king. He even has a castle. It's a boarded-up, wildly painted gazebo in his backyard. The boards are there to keep the rain from blowing in and the paint forms vivid psychedelic rainbows inside. At the end of each rainbow is Harvey Trumble's treasure, beer cans.

"Harvey has a big collection of beer cans stacked all around his castle, which he decorated with the help of two neighbor boys he calls his 'trusty knights,' Billy Leonard and Simon Kelly. 'They're little kids who like to work for me,' Harveys says."

I groaned out loud. I couldn't believe I had said that. But I remembered how much I wanted to keep Karen Gray interested during that interview. I could have said anything. Billy and Simon are going to explode, I thought. It's going to be worse than eggs this time.

" 'A lot of my cans are really rare,' " the article went on. It hurt my head to read it, but I couldn't stop. " 'I have a fabulous collection,' Harvey points out. The cans in his gazebo have such names as Royal Bohemian, Regal, and Rex. 'I really had to work hard to find great ones like that,' Harvey told me."

"Good grief," I moaned. Those were the cans I got from Billy and Simon. They were the cans we'd given

Suzanna. And there I was in the paper, big-dealing about how hard *I'd* worked to get them. I considered crawling under the front porch and staying there a week or two. But I read on.

" 'I'm fantastic at this,' the eleven-year-old collector said, leaning back in his gilded grapefruit-crate throne."

"Not eleven, *twelve!*" I shouted. "I'm twelve. Can't she get anything right?"

" 'And I bet I've got more cans than anybody in town.' Harvey has 'somewhere between six and seven hundred good ones.' He thinks it's the best hobby there is because 'I help keep the world clean by picking up junk.' If he keeps going, Harvey Trumble could well become a Beer Can King."

Right now, I thought, people all over Pittsfield are reading this article and they're laughing like crazy. All except Billy and Simon, and they're not laughing at all. I could just imagine what it would be like when Suzanna's dad got back in town and saw how many cans I thought was a stupendous collection.

That article was like one of those magazine stories you read about movie stars and you just know you wouldn't like them if you met them. Only it was about *me*. And all the things I didn't like the most were in quotation marks. It was me that said them.

"Harvey," Peter yelled. "Somebody wants to talk to you on the telephone."

97

"I'm busy," I told him. I didn't want to hear what anybody had to say. "Take a message."

I waited, thinking it couldn't be anything good. Pete stuck his head in the living room. "It was Mr. Grundle," he said, "the guy who owns that new Hobby Hutch. He wonders if you'd stop by and see him. He'd like to talk to you about beer cans." Pete looked over my shoulder and saw my picture. "Hey, that's you, kid. Congratulations," he said, lifting the paper out of my hands.

As quick as I could, I got out of there. I decided I might as well go over and see what Mr. Grundle wanted. I'd only been in his place once and it didn't look half bad.

I took the skateboard, whizzing along past everybody. I didn't stop once, except at curbs.

Mr. Grundle was in, and about ten little kids were milling around the train that he'd set up in the middle of the store. They were poking at things, but nobody was buying. Mr. Grundle looked up from the train display.

"Why, Harvey," he said, "you sure got here in a hurry. Did your mother drive you?"

"No," I told him. "I rode my skateboard. How'd you know I was Harvey?"

"I saw your picture in the paper," he said. "It said you know a lot about cans. And I don't. I bought this collection from my cousin. He said it might bring kids into the store. But cans take up too much space. I'm just going to see if I can sell what I have here.

98

I don't plan to get any more." He looked up at the shelf of cans and shook his head. "The trouble is I don't know how to price these. I thought maybe you could help me. The prices my cousin said I should charge are just too high. No kid's going to pay twelve dollars for a can."

"Don't price them too low, either," I warned him. "I can help you out some, but Suzanna Brooks and her father have got a much bigger collection than I do and they go to beer-can conventions and everything. They can give you better advice than I can."

"I thought you had the biggest collection in town," Mr. Grundle said, kind of surprised.

"So did I," I told him.

Mr. Grundle turned away to help this little kid who wanted to buy a Pearl beer can that was up on the shelf. "What do you think, Harvey?" he asked me. "How much?"

I looked it over. "It's got a scratch on it," I told him. "I'd give it to her for a quarter."

"Twenty-five cents, young lady," he said. The kid seemed pretty pleased, and I asked her how many cans she had at home.

"Forty-three," she told me. "This one makes forty-four."

I turned to Mr. Grundle. "So you don't want to buy my cans?" I asked him.

"Buy them?" He hadn't expected that. "Why do you want to sell them?"

"Oh, I don't know," I shrugged. I started to say

that I'd found out somebody else had more, but that sounded stupid. Because I'd made a dumb trade? That didn't sound like a good reason either. "I don't know," was all I could think of.

"There are a lot of kids come in here wanting to trade beer cans with me," he said, nodding toward his beer-can display. "Why don't you start a club, Harvey? You could get all the collectors together so they could trade with each other. You could make lists of what everybody's got and what they want to trade. I think they'd like that a lot. Maybe you could even build your collection that way." He walked over and told some little kid not to take the train off the track.

"I'll think about that," I called to him. "I really will. But you better talk to the Brookses about the prices. Thanks a lot, Mr. Grundle."

I was feeling better when I swung open the door to walk out. He'd really wanted my advice on beer cans. But standing right out in front, eating cherry snow cones, were Billy, Simon, and a couple of their friends. I got goosebumps on my neck imagining what a cherry snow cone would feel like melting down my spine.

"Well," Simon said, "if it isn't the King Kan Monster. Want some snow cone, King?" He grinned and faked a big windup with his cone.

"You must have seen the paper," I said.

"Yeah," Billy answered. "My mother said it sounded like we were your slaves or something."

"I didn't say it like that," I said. "The reporter got it all wrong. Maybe she said that stuff because you got her in the face with an egg. Think what your mom would have said if *that* had got in the paper." It was probably hitting below the belt to get them with that, but it worked. Even Simon didn't know what to say.

"Anyway, we're making signs for Eric Wagner," Billy said. "They say, 'Wagner's a Superskate.'"

"That's not fair," I said. "You can't even vote. You're not in the sixth grade."

"We can't vote, but we can make signs if we want to," Billy said. "We watched him go down Suicide Hill doing stunts. He's a pro."

Just then, Quint rode up at full speed on his bike. When he braked he left a skid line a meter long. "Well," he said, "I see you guys are getting the truth about beer cans from 'The Boy Who Would Be King.'"

"Sure," I said, "why not? And how's the Kid with the Cat on his Neck?"

"Ah, that's not the question," he said. "The question is, 'How's the guy on the skateboard?' Did you hear?"

"No," I said. "Hear what?"

"Eric Wagner was skateboarding right-side-up down his driveway after school. He hit this crack and crashed. His brother says he's at the hospital with a broken collarbone." He smiled that smirky smile. "We may be the only two guys running tomorrow,

Monster. Just me and the Beer Can Cheat. And just wait'll you hear what I say about you in my speech."

He got on his bike and sped away.

11 · X Marks the Ballot

The day of the contest it was raining. It was kind of dark and you could see the lights in the classrooms from three blocks away. I stood for a minute outside school with the water running off my yellow poncho, wondering if I should go back home and say I was sick. I looked up at the *1948* cast in concrete in the arch over the big front door. It was right below my homeroom on the second floor, and there were already kids standing by the window at the pencil sharpener. The school bus was pulling up, bringing kids in from the country, and the rain was coming down harder, so I decided to go in.

I chucked the poncho in my locker. In the hall there were lots of notebook-paper signs written with felt-tip pens. Stuff like "Suzanna Brooks Is Super Great. She's So Fast She's Never Late." And "Anne Wilson, Swimmer—Is a Winner." Some of them had rhymes that would make you gag. I saw one of the circus kids with a "De-Throne King Kan. Quint's Our Man" sign that sounded like Quint had written it. There was a "Harvey Drinks" sign. I tore it down and crumpled it up.

"Hey, Harv," somebody called. I looked around

and saw Tom Andrews, Matt Marrinson, and a couple of other kids hanging around the new trophy case in the front hall. It had this big sheet of glass in front, a couple of empty shelves, and an overhead light that wasn't plugged in yet. It had real possibilities. Down on his knees, in front of it, the janitor was hammering a little brass plate on the bottom edge of the case.

"How's it going?" Matt asked me.

"It's going great," I lied. "What's that thing say?"

"Just some junk about the *Examiner* donating it," he said, shrugging.

"This'll really be a good place for Field Day trophies, no joke," Tom was telling somebody. "Our homeroom got one for high points last spring and then they kept the thing in the principal's office all year long."

"He didn't run anything but the stopwatch. Why should he get to keep it?" Matt turned around to me. "Your name gonna be on one of the first two trophies in here, Harv?"

"Sure," I told him. "Sure it is. If you guys vote for me."

"Count on me," Matt said.

"Yeah, well, see you around, Harv," Tom muttered and wandered off.

I could tell I was going to have to stir up some votes, so I walked on down the hall with a politician's smile, saying hello to everybody, even the girls all clustered around their lockers.

Billy and Simon were taping up one of their "Eric Wagner, Superskate" posters next to the gym.

"Hey, you guys," I called. "I talked to Eric's mother last night on the phone. She says he's gotta be in the hospital a couple of days."

Quint came rushing up and tried to shoulder me away. "I don't see how you little kids can put up posters for Eric after all I've done for you," he said. "Besides, he's not running anymore."

"Isn't Eric gonna be in the contest?" Billy asked.

"It's not fair if he can't," Simon said.

"There's nothing in the rules that says he has to be here," I said, trying to remember what the rules said.

"That shows how much you know. I just read the rules again," Quint announced. "They say that the sixth-graders vote after they've heard the finalists speak. I say that unless Eric is on the stage this afternoon, he's not in the contest. That's what I say."

"Quentin Calkins, you're a creep," I growled. "I'm gonna see to it that you lose this contest."

Quint laughed. "Look who's talking," he said as loud as he could. He tried to get the kids walking down the hall to listen to him. "This kid who cheats third-graders when he's trading beer cans . . ."

"He's not all that bad," Simon cut in.

"Besides, we're big enough to take care of ourselves," Billy added.

"He cheats little kids," Quint shouted on, unstoppable, "breaks up my circus . . ." Kids started hanging around to listen, hoping, I guess, for a fight.

"The rain did that," I said.

"Cheats little kids, breaks up my circus, brags like a fool in the paper about a really nothing beer-can collection . . ."

I couldn't think of anything to say to that one. It was true.

"And King Kan says he's gonna see to it that *I* don't win this contest. You're not going to have anybody voting for you, buddy. So you're not going to keep me from doing anything. All I've got to do is give my talk, read the rules about how the finalists have to give speeches, and it's you against me. After I say a few choice things about you, I give you one guess who gets his name engraved on a trophy."

"I may not win," I told him, trying to stare him down, "but you won't either."

"You sound pretty sure of yourself," Quint said as he strolled off down the hall. "What'd you do? Bring your handy-dandy gerbils to school with you?"

"I don't like Quint anymore," Simon said, picking up his books.

"Me neither," Billy agreed.

"Yeah," I said, "but you're not voting this afternoon. I've gotta think of something to do. I may not be so great, but he's the least Superkid I know." And I hurried off down the hall.

Suzanna was walking along with a gang of girls,

some of them waving Suzanna signs. "We're voting for you, Harvey," Suzanna called to me.

"I'm not," said one of the other girls.

"Well, I am," Suzanna announced. "See you later, Harv."

I sat down on the bench where the kids wait to go into the office, under the big picture of George Washington. I had to figure out what I was going to do. Quint was going around calling me a bragger and a cheat. The circus kids were still mad, and I couldn't prove I didn't let my gerbil go on purpose. I was just sitting there looking at nothing, waiting for some bright idea, when the principal, Mr. Healy, tapped me on the shoulder and said, "Did somebody send you to the office, Harvey?"

Mr. Healy's way over six feet and he towered over me, looking grim. I could tell he didn't know whether to be nice to me or treat me like I had just been caught dropping a water balloon out the window.

"No, no, sir," I said, jumping up. "Just resting."

"Getting ready for your big talk this afternoon? Well, now, I expect you'd like to have a big case like our new one to display your collection, wouldn't you?" he asked. His little brown moustache twitched.

"Oh, sure, yes, I would." The bell rang, so I picked up my books and headed upstairs toward homeroom.

At two o'clock all the fourth-, fifth-, and sixth-graders filed into the auditorium for the assembly to hear the finalists. Since Eric was still in the hospital,

107

there were just five of us kids on the stage. The footlights were on and we couldn't see much on the other
side of them. You could sure hear all those kids,
though. It sounded like a waterfall.

I had a speech written down on three-by-five cards.
I'd written it the night before. It was about beer cans.
I hadn't known what to say, so I put down what my
dad suggested—stuff from a book, mostly, about the
history of beer cans. Ho, hum. That's ten votes right
there, I figured—the teachers and Mr. Healy. Except
they can't vote. I folded the cards up, stuck them in
my back pocket, and started to panic.

Everybody got quiet. A couple of Girl Scouts led
the Pledge, and we all sang "America the Beautiful."
Then the fourth-grade chorus lined up in front of
the stage and got through "This Land is Your Land"
and something else I forgot to listen to. Before I knew
it, Mr. Healy bounded up the stage steps, stood at
the microphone, and raised it about four feet. I
blinked, trying to see past the footlights.

"Boys and girls," he said. You could hear his voice
booming over the PA system. "This is a special day
for Central School. Today we are receiving a very
useful and decorative gift from the Pittsfield *Examiner*. How many of you have seen the new display
case in the front hall?"

Everybody raised their hands. I mean, you couldn't
have missed it, really. It was right out there.

"Now," he went on, "I knew that all of the children
involved in competing for trophies on Field Day—

all the fourth-, fifth-, and sixth-graders—would espe-
cially want to be here to express their thanks. People,
I want you to give our very finest welcome to the man
who is responsible for giving us such a fine present—
the president of our local Lions Club, Editor-in-Chief
of the *Examiner,* and our good friend, Mr. George
Adams."

They clapped pretty hard, and I expect Mr. Adams
felt good about the whole thing because, after he low-
ered the mike, he talked on and on about how every-
one in this fine auditorium is a good sport and a super
kid and how he'd thought about this whole thing
one day when he saw the trophies sitting on a shelf
in the principal's office. Then he held up these two
gold cups and said everybody deserved them but that
he was certainly looking forward to the speeches of
the fine young people who were the finalists.

I wasn't, but I was glad, anyway, when he sat down.

The girls talked first. The first two told about how
great they were at home, at school, at play, in the
community, in the nation, in the world, in the uni-
verse. Boy, was I getting bored. Suzanna was different.
She unicycled up to the front of the stage and got
a big hand. She gave her whole talk, which was short,
while she rode on the unicycle. She didn't even use
the microphone. Everybody liked it. Mr. Adams was
smiling his head off. You could tell he thought those
girls were "fine young people."

Quint was next. He was nervous. While everybody
talked, he'd been bending his cards back and forth,

and they were a mess. I guess he must not have realized it because when he held them up to read from them, he looked pretty shocked.

"Fellow sixth-graders," he said, "and all you fourth- and fifth-graders, too." Then he turned around and looked at me with that big phony smile. "I guess Harvey Trumble and me are the only two boys running in this contest."

You could hear a murmur out in the auditorium. The kids must have wondered what he was up to. "Last night I read the rules for this contest again," he went on, "and they say . . ." He shuffled through his cards, found the one he wanted, and started to read from it. " 'The winners will be chosen by a vote of the Central School sixth-graders on Tuesday, May 18, after an assembly at which the finalists will speak.' That means that since Eric can't speak at this assembly, he can't be in the contest."

The buzz in the audience got louder. Mr. Adams frowned and leaned over to talk to Mr. Healy, so I don't think they heard Quint when he said, "You should vote for me instead of Harvey because he cheats when he trades cans from his little collection, because . . ." The audience was really rumbling by then. I grabbed hold of the edge of my chair. I couldn't let him get away with that. Some guys in front were booing and I could see my homeroom teacher, Mrs. Faris, stand up and try to quiet the class. Even Quint could tell he'd gone too far. He suddenly started talking fast about his back-yard circus and his community spirit, but the mumbling went on.

Mr. Healy stood up. "All right, people!" he boomed. "I don't want to have to talk to you about rude behavior today. Give Quentin your attention."

As soon as Mr. Healy sat down, Quint threw his hands out wide and the long black cane appeared in one of them, just like it did at his circus. It was still a good trick and got a laugh.

"So," he shouted into the mike, "now that you know who to vote for . . ." He drew a big fake gun out of his pocket. "I'm going to leave you with a . . ." He pointed the gun offstage, Mr. Healy got an anxious look on his face, and everybody waited for some kind of explosion. But when he pulled the trigger a flag dropped down. *BANG*, it said. A lot of kids laughed. Some of them clapped. Quint bowed like a magician and sat down. The question was, were they clapping for him or his tricks?

It was my turn. My hands were just pouring sweat and I wasn't sure my knees would make it to the microphone. I put my cards on the stand and looked out. At the microphone I could finally see all those kids staring up at me. I glanced back down at the cards. "I am very proud to be a finalist in this contest," I read, realizing all along that I was saying each word separate—like little kids read. I wiped my palms on the seat of my jeans and looked up again. "I collect beer cans," I said.

"He collects gerbils, too." I heard a girl giggle.

111

I looked around at Quint and saw him grinning. Mrs. Faris said, "Shush."

"Well, anyway." I went on reading my cards. "I found out in a book about beer cans that they started manufacturing them in 1935 and that now there are a quarter of a million beer-can collectors in this country. First, they were made of . . . of . . ." I lost my place and squinted at my cards. The lights were hot, and it felt like a hundred degrees. My hands were still sweating and my throat was dry as sand. I could feel the panic building up again.

Quint coughed. I could hear him behind me. The kids were really restless, talking and shuffling their feet. I looked down again and opened my mouth. Nothing came out. Then, all of a sudden, the cards slipped through my hands and fell on the floor. They scattered all over, and one or two even fell off the stage. Quint broke up. The kids roared, all of them. It went on forever. I wanted to go back to the gazebo.

I picked the cards up, one by one, but it was hopeless. I'd never find my place again. It was all over for me. Eric sure was one lucky kid not having to stand up here and talk. I'd rather bust my shoulder any old day. Anyway, I thought, it was stupid that Eric couldn't win.

Then it dawned on me that it was *too* stupid, that I could *make* him win if I wanted to. I wouldn't get a trophy, but I could keep Quint from walking off with one.

I just stood there waiting, not feeling like I was in a steam bath anymore. Finally, the kids stopped laughing. I guess they were wondering what I'd say next.

I held onto the stand and leaned over to the microphone. "Listen, I've got a good idea. Instead of voting for me, maybe you should vote for Eric Wagner. The

only reason he's not here is that he's in the hospital with a broken collarbone." There were a few whispers, but then it got very, very quiet. They were listening.

"I'll speak for Eric," I said—slow, because I wasn't sure what to say next. "He's a real pro on the skateboard. And a nice guy. And I don't see any reason why a bad accident like he had should keep him from winning the contest, do you?" I turned around to look at Quint. He was green.

There was a lot of clapping. They liked it. Somehow, I'd said the right thing. I didn't know whether to be happy or sick. Then they stopped clapping and waited again.

"I want to take this opportunity," I went on, trying to sound official instead of defeated, "to say that anybody who'd like to belong to a beer-can collectors' club should meet me—in front of the Hobby Hutch this afternoon—at three-thirty." I looked down, grabbed my unused cards, and mumbled, ". . . and maybe I can be president of that."

When I sat down there was a lot of talking and some more clapping and Quint leaned over and said, "Harvey Trumble, you are a rat, a sneaky rotten rat."

"Thanks," I said, and smiled out at the audience.

Mr. Healy walked over to the mike. "Boys and girls," he said. Nothing happened. "All right, now, people. I know this is an exciting time for you, but I'd like your attention. Mr. Adams and I have been talking." He glanced over to Mr. Adams, who nodded. "And we feel that while it may be *strictly* true, according to the rules, that Eric should be here in order to qualify, we know you all agree that our good sportsmanship should allow Eric to be a contestant. You were right about that, Harvey," he said, and smiled at me.

"So, if the teachers will please pass out ballots to the sixth-graders, they may vote. Mark an X by the name of one boy and one girl."

They even passed out ballots on the stage. I couldn't help it. I voted for myself. And for Suzanna.

While they counted the votes, we had to sing. I guess it was to keep us from talking. Before they finished adding them up we'd gotten through "On Top of Old Smoky," which almost everybody sings "On Top of Spaghetti," and then a couple of rounds of "Row, Row, Row Your Boat" which the little kids always turn into "Propel, Propel, Propel Your Craft." I don't know why it should take so long to count ninety-three ballots.

Mr. Adams made the announcement. He stepped up to the mike carrying the trophies and a piece of paper. "The results are in," he said, beaming. "These two trophies go into Nielsen's Jewelers this very afternoon to have names engraved on them, names of the two sixth-graders you have chosen to be winners of our Superkids Contest." Then he paused, just to make us wait. "And *then* the trophies will be placed in the brand new trophy case." He paused again, and you could tell then that he was playing this kind of game with us, dangling us along, that he still wasn't going to announce it right away. "And *then* after next week's Field Day, there'll be even more awards for the glass case." He waited again, liking all that suspense. Kids began to giggle. "Well, I guess it's time to announce the winners. It gives me great personal pleasure to introduce the young lady who received the most votes, an *Examiner* paper carrier—Miss Suzanna Brooks. Let's have a nice hand for Suzanna." Suzanna stood up and gave a little wave to the audience.

"Way to go, Suzanna!" somebody yelled.

"And the young man who won—is going to be mighty happy to hear about this in his hospital bed. It's Eric Wagner."

And that was that. I don't know whether I did the right thing or not. I felt kind of noble, telling everybody they should vote for a sick kid in the hospital. That was *very* nice of me, I thought. I honestly did feel like a good guy. I even wondered once or twice why somebody as good as I am wasn't elected Superkid after all.

12 · Hirshvogel

I got to the Hobby Hutch as soon as I could, around 3:25. The rain had stopped, but there were lots of puddles in the street. A crowd of kids had gathered. Some of them were talking about the contest. "Hey, Harv," one guy said, "you should have stuck in there. Maybe you'd have won." Maybe. Maybe I would have.

Billy and Simon came splashing through the puddles, snickering like they'd just won the lottery.

"We've found out what to do with beer cans," Billy yelled.

"Yeah, my mom told us about it," Simon said. "She told us about these guys who made a boat out of 15,000 beer cans . . ."

". . . and sailed it," Billy cut in, "from Australia to Singapore."

"No joke. They called it the *Can-Tiki*. We figure we could build one."

"We could make it out of 15,001 cans and get in *The Guinness Book of World Records*."

"And we could call it the *CANnibal* . . ."

"Or the *CANoe* . . ."

"And sail it to *Can*ada . . ."

"Up the *can*al . . ."

"I can't stand it," I yelled. "Enough, enough."

"Can we belong to your can club?" Simon asked.

"Well, why not." I was going to have to watch those guys. I really was.

At least twenty kids showed up. They were telling each other about their conies and flip-tops, deciding whether they wanted to trade a Dixie Light for a Velvet Glove Malt and wondering whether a kid's Burgermeister eleven-ounce was really worth five-to-one. Well, it wasn't winning, but it was something.

I got them all together, told them where I lived, and asked them to come to the gazebo next Saturday at two o'clock for our first meeting. "We'll make lists of the cans we want to trade," I told them, "and we can clean up the parks and get more cans and go searching in the lake on hot days. It'll be a great club.

"Now all you guys bring lists of your cans Saturday, doubles and all," I was saying, when Suzanna came whizzing round the corner on her unicycle. "Congratulations again," I called to her. "I knew you'd win."

"Thanks," she said. "You were great, Harvey. Don't go away. My dad wants to see you."

I was in for it. I just knew it. Suzanna's dad had read that article in the paper. He was going to tell me what a dumb kid I was for spouting off about how I was the greatest when I wasn't. My dad had already told me that. "You've got to stop bragging, Harvey," he said. "One, you can't go around saying you're the best at something unless you really are. Two, even if you are the best, you shouldn't say so yourself. Three, you ought to know that a batch of beer cans can't make you a king. Beer cans are just beer cans."

So I was all ready for Suzanna's dad to give me Father Lecture Number Two when he came jogging around the corner. Suzanna leaned her unicycle against a parking meter and brought him over to me.

"This is Harvey Trumble, Dad," she said.

Mr. Brooks looked me over. "So this is the Beer Can King," he said.

"Oh, no, sir," I told him. "I really didn't mean to say all that about being great and terrific. I honestly didn't know until after I talked to the reporter that you and Suzanna have a lot more cans than I do." I hoped he would just say, OK, kid, that's all right, but don't let it happen again.

"Well, Suzanna, she's the one. She keeps me out there turning up cans. It gets to you, though, like peanuts. You just can't stop searching. So, Harvey, *our* collection . . ." I tried to close my ears off so the lecture wouldn't come through so strong. "Our collection is bigger than yours," he went on, and I thought maybe he'd even start listing his biggies. "But yours just might be better."

I didn't know what he was talking about. He'd never even seen my cans. And neither had Suzanna. Then I remembered the conies we'd given her. I figured he must have thought they were doubles from my collection. Some fantastic doubles those would have been.

"Oh, you mean those conies," I said. "We gave those to Suzanna. They weren't doubles or anything, though. I'm glad you like them. They're pretty rich."

Simon heard the talk about conies and sidled up to listen.

"I figure you for a pretty smart kid, Harvey," Mr. Brooks told me. "And smart kids don't give good conies away—even to girls who are hotshots on the unicycle." He smiled over at Suzanna like he thought she was really great. "Look, Suze and I'll drop them by your house tonight—if you and your folks are going to be home."

"And *we'll* pick them up in the morning," Simon said to me. "If Billy and me are going to belong to this club, we're going to start out with first-rate cans. You want that bag of doubles back?"

"They're yours," I said, "all of them. So long as you promise not to try sailing the Atlantic in them."

Mr. Brooks reached in his jacket and took out the newspaper with our pictures on the front page. "It isn't those conies at all, Harvey. First thing I saw in the paper—after Suzanna on her unicycle—was this Hirshvogel quart conie," he said, pointing to the can I was holding in the picture. Then he laughed. "You really don't know about that Hirshvogel, do you?"

"The Hirshvogel?" I asked him. Maybe I had been wrong to tell Mr. Grundle that Mr. Brooks knew so much. He didn't know what he was talking about. "There's nothing to know about the Hirshvogel. It's *nothing*. I've never even seen it in a beer-can book. It isn't worth anything."

"Mind my asking where you found it?"

"It was kind of weird, really," I told him. "It was over at the car graveyard where they've got all those old wrecks. You know, Steve's Body Shop out on Route 13?" He nodded. The place is a big eyesore, my dad says, but it's been there for years on the outskirts of town. "Dad was looking for a fender out there last summer and I went with him. I found the Hirshvogel in the glove compartment of a really broken-down old Ford. I found a flashlight, too, but it didn't work."

"Harvey, I guess you're not going to believe this. But you did it. You really did. Let me just tell you about that Hirshvogel," Mr. Brooks said. "A couple of years ago, my friend Al Bolan and me, we were at a beer-can collectors' convention. We met this old fellow, name of Heinrich Hirshvogel, used to own a very small brewery in a very small Wisconsin town, he said. He'd closed the place in the forties, during the Second World War. He just gave it up and moved to Chicago to live with his brother's family."

The kids had all gathered round to listen to Mr. Brooks. I still wasn't sure what it was adding up to, but at least I knew he wasn't mad at me.

"The old man," he went on, "came to the convention hoping to locate one of his cans. He hadn't kept

121

any. Imagine that. I guess hardly anybody kept cans in those days just for the sake of collecting them. Besides, it wasn't much of a brewery, so there weren't all that many cans in the first place. But Hirshvogel wanted one in the worst way. Just to have as a keepsake. Nobody had one. None of those collectors had even heard of Hirshvogel. The poor guy went around shaking hands and saying, 'Don't you know where I can find one of my lost Hirshvogel cans?' But nobody knew."

"You mean," I asked him, "that nobody's found one yet? The one I have is all there is?"

"I was right that you're smart," Mr. Brooks said, smiling very big. "That's about it. The beer-can magazine I get has an ad every once in a while asking if somebody's found one. People are always after things they can't have. They don't even have a photograph, just a sketch that the old man made of a blue-and-white can—steel, he said—with a gold bird above the word *Hirshvogel* on one side and a golden deer on the other."

"That's what it looks like, all right," I admitted. "But I don't think it's any big deal. It doesn't look *that* old."

"Ah," he went on, waving the newspaper in the air. "That's the thing about old cans—those made in the late thirties and very early forties. The thing about them is that they were made of heavy steel and covered with good thick labels. They were made to *last*. You see, Harvey, an old can sometimes looks a lot newer than a new one."

"But why isn't it in any of the books, Dad?" Suzanna asked, taking the newspaper from him and looking at it closely. All the other kids gathered round the paper.

Tom Andrews wandered over with a snow cone and looked at the picture. "That's nothing," he said, shrugging his shoulders. "I've seen one like that before." Mr. Brooks looked over at him, amazed. "Well, sort of like that," he said, and moved around behind a tall kid.

"Maybe it wasn't listed because nobody knows how much it's worth," Mr. Brooks said. "Soon as I saw that picture of you and the Hirshvogel this morning, Harvey, I went down to the newspaper office to get a better look. I told them about the can. Hope you don't mind. Anyway, right from the newspaper I called this man who's a big collector in Kenosha. He said if that can's the real thing, he'll give you five hundred dollars for it."

"Five hundred dollars!" I yelped. This guy is crazy, I thought. What else could I think? "There isn't a beer can anywhere worth five hundred dollars."

"Probably not." He laughed. "But I know somebody who's offered to pay you that. Personally, I'd hold onto it. You might get a better offer."

Peter came racing up on his bike. "Hey, Harvey, that reporter, Karen Gray, has been trying to reach

you on the phone. Mom said I should try to find you."
He rode over to me and joined the gang who'd been
listening to Mr. Brooks. "She told Mom that some
other papers were going to print that picture of you
and the beer can. She says one of your cans is worth
a lot of money. She told Mom you're famous."

I choked and somebody had to hit me on the back
to help me get my breath.

"You didn't believe me, did you, Harvey?" Mr.
Brooks laughed.

"Is my brother a millionaire or something?" Peter
asked.

"He must feel like one," Mr. Brooks said.

"But, Dad," Suzanna asked, "what about Mr.
Hirshvogel? Won't he want the can?" I'd been wondering the same thing.

"No," he said. "The old man died last year on a
trip to Germany. But I'll bet he would have been
plenty pleased that Harvey here found one of his
cans."

"Grab on, Harvey, I'll pull you home," Peter said,
tossing me the tow rope we keep tied to the bike seat.
"Mom's probably still talking to that reporter, trying
to find out what's going on."

I got on my skateboard and grabbed the rope, feeling as if somebody had beaned me on the head with
a baseball. "Thanks a lot, Mr. Brooks," I said. "I
might have thrown that Hirshvogel away, or something."

"Glad to be the one to tell you," he said. "But I

124

sure want to see it firsthand. Suze and I'll stop by this evening."

As we rode off, Peter said, "Hey, Harvey, I'm sorry you didn't win the contest."

"It doesn't matter," I told him. "It really doesn't matter."

The phone rang the minute I got inside the house. "That's Karen Gray," my mother said. "She keeps calling. I hope she's not playing a joke on you because of that egg she got hit with."

Mom was right. It was Karen Gray. She was telling me the same stuff Mr. Brooks had told me about the Hirshvogel being so rare when my dad came rushing in the front door.

"Harvey, is it true?" he asked. "Somebody just came in the store and told me you'd been offered five hundred dollars for a beer can!"

I told Karen Gray to hold on for a minute. "Sure, it's true," I told him. "I'm talking to a reporter about it right now."

"Listen, Harvey," he said quick, like it was really urgent, "I found this can on the way home." He held up a shiny new Old Chicago. "What do you think?" he asked me. "Shall we keep it?"

"Sure," I told him. "You never can tell what it's gonna be worth in a couple of years." I could hardly wait for him to meet Mr. Brooks.

"Hey, thanks for calling," I told Karen Gray. "I've got to go now."

"No, wait," she said. "I haven't come to the best

part. I really called to tell you that the wire service picked up your picture and the five hundred-dollar can story."

"Wire service?" I asked her.

"It's a service for newspapers," she said. "They send pictures all over the world, pictures of people in the news. Today, that's you, Harvey. You're news."

All over the world? Maybe the President of the United States would see my picture. Maybe the Emperor of Japan. Maybe the Queen of England would pick up her morning paper and there I'd be on the front page. "What's it look like?" I asked her.

"Well, it's that picture of you wearing your crown, holding out the can of Hirshvogel. And under it there's a paragraph about you with a heading you're really going to like."

"What's it say?" I asked.

"It says," she told me, "Harvey, the Beer Can King."

"Harvey, the Beer Can King," printed in newspapers all over the world. Harvey, the Beer Can King!

On the Fourth of July I bet they'll let me have my own float in the parade. Gold with rainbows. I'll sit on a huge throne on top and I'll wave at everybody lined up and down Lake Street. They have floats for queens all the time. Beauty queens, that's nothing. Harvey, the Beer Can King, now that's really worth a float. And once it's dark, there'll be fireworks like always. Only this year there's got to be a fireworks crown. They'll light it from the bottom and it'll slowly catch fire, fizz, and sparkle until the whole crown is flashing gold and silver. Then, POW! all at once, the words on top of it will explode in a blaze of gold. I could see it. In fireworks, *Harvey, the Beer Can King.*

"Harvey! Harvey, are you there? Are you OK?" Karen Gray was saying.

"Sure, I'm OK," I said. "I sure am." And I hung up. I could feel myself grinning.